SO-AZZ-046

"How could I live in the same house with a female like you and not want you?" Rusty said.

"You're beautiful," he continued. "And all woman."

Stunned, Lucy kept her head down. "Please," she said belatedly, "don't say those things."

"Why not?"

"Because I can't. I didn't come to the Lazy S for that. I want a family, Rusty."

"Family," he echoed in disbelief. "You mean you want to treat me like some kind of...of brother?"

At least he understood, she thought, relieved. She nodded firmly. "Yes. A brother."

Surprising her, he threw back his head and guffawed. "Woman, I think maybe you've lost a few head of cattle from your herd." His laughter filled the fall air. "There's nothing brotherly about the way I feel about you, Lucy. And you're not being truthful with your own feelings if you say you think of *me* that way."

Dear Reader,

As spring turns to summer, make Silhouette Romance the perfect companion for those lazy days and sultry nights! Fans of our LOVING THE BOSS series won't want to miss *The Marriage Merger* by exciting author Vivian Leiber. A pretend engagement between friends goes awry when their white lies lead to a *real* white wedding!

Take one biological-clock-ticking twin posing as a new mom and one daddy determined to gain custody of his newborn son, and you've got the unsuspecting partners in *The Baby Arrangement,* Moyra Tarling's tender BUNDLES OF JOY title. You've asked for more TWINS ON THE DOORSTEP, Stella Bagwell's charming author-led miniseries, so this month we give you *Millionaire on Her Doorstep,* an emotional story of two wounded souls who find love in the most unexpected way...and in the most unexpected place.

Can a bachelor bent on never marrying and a single mom with a bustling brood of four become a *Fairy-Tale Family?* Find out in Pat Montana's delightful new novel. Next, a handsome doctor's case of mistaken identity leads to *The Triplet's Wedding Wish* in this heartwarming tale by DeAnna Talcott. And a young widow finds the home—and family—she's always wanted when she strikes a deal with a *Nevada Cowboy Dad,* this month's FAMILY MATTERS offering from Dorsey Kelley.

Enjoy this month's fantastic selections, and make sure to return each and every month to Silhouette Romance!

Mary-Theresa Hussey

Mary-Theresa Hussey
Senior Editor, Silhouette Romance

Please address questions and book requests to:
Silhouette Reader Service
U.S.: 3010 Walden Ave., P.O. Box 1325, Buffalo, NY 14269
Canadian: P.O. Box 609, Fort Erie, Ont. L2A 5X3

NEVADA
COWBOY DAD

Dorsey Kelley

Silhouette
R O M A N C E™
Published by Silhouette Books
America's Publisher of Contemporary Romance

If you purchased this book without a cover you should be aware
that this book is stolen property. It was reported as "unsold and
destroyed" to the publisher, and neither the author nor the
publisher has received any payment for this "stripped book."

I dedicate this novel to all the fine organizations
that support verbally abused and physically
battered women, and most especially to the
Nicole Brown Simpson Charitable Foundation.
For any abused wife: Please, take heart, and get help.

 SILHOUETTE BOOKS

ISBN 0-373-19371-8

NEVADA COWBOY DAD

Copyright © 1999 by Dorsey Adams

All rights reserved. Except for use in any review, the reproduction
or utilization of this work in whole or in part in any form by any
electronic, mechanical or other means, now known or hereafter
invented, including xerography, photocopying and recording, or in
any information storage or retrieval system, is forbidden without
the written permission of the editorial office, Silhouette Books,
300 East 42nd Street, New York, NY 10017 U.S.A.

All characters in this book have no existence outside the imagination of
the author and have no relation whatsoever to anyone bearing the same
name or names. They are not even distantly inspired by any individual
known or unknown to the author, and all incidents are pure invention.

This edition published by arrangement with Harlequin Books S.A.

® and TM are trademarks of Harlequin Books S.A., used under license.
Trademarks indicated with ® are registered in the United States Patent
and Trademark Office, the Canadian Trade Marks Office and in other
countries.

Look us up on-line at: http://www.romance.net

Printed in U.S.A.

Books by Dorsey Kelley

Silhouette Romance

Montana Heat #714
Lone Star Man #863
Texas Maverick #900
Wrangler #938
The Cowboy's Proposal #997
Cowboy for Hire #1098
Nevada Cowboy Dad #1371

DORSEY KELLEY

can hardly get off a horse long enough to write books. She helps ranchers move cattle around in annual drives, participates in roundups and brandings and hams it up in parades. Now she is learning to team rope because, she says, "It's so darn much fun!"

When she isn't horsing around, Dorsey plays tennis, takes her three daughters to the mall and makes her husband crazy with planning even more ranch trips.

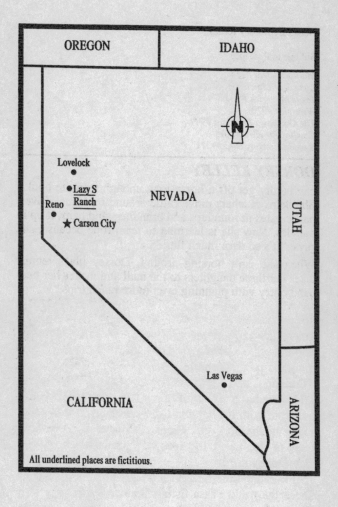

OREGON

IDAHO

N

Lovelock

Lazy S Ranch

Reno

NEVADA

UTAH

★ Carson City

Las Vegas

CALIFORNIA

ARIZONA

All underlined places are fictitious.

Chapter One

She was coming back. And she was bringing her money with her.

That was all Rusty Sheffield allowed himself to think about as he waited on horseback for the sleek sports car to make its way up the gravel drive of the Lazy S Ranch. The expensive engine almost purred, he thought broodingly, as out of place on the Nevada cattle ranch as antlers on a sheepdog.

Impatient and frustrated, Rusty yanked off his hat and slapped at a clump of dried mud on his thigh. Dust rose from both his hat and his worn jeans, making thin clouds in the chill air. *Damn,* he hated what he was about to do, hated the reason for this meeting with Lucy Donovan.

Still, every time he reviewed the ranch's dismal finances the truth was a fist slamming agonizingly into his gut. He resettled his hat, but there was no denying it—he was getting desperate.

Lifting the reins, he urged his sorrel gelding out the

corral and toward the gravelled area where Lucy had parked her car and was now emerging.

"Welcome back." He touched his Stetson and forced out the courtesy. "It's been a long time."

Lucy lingered in the embrace of her car's door, blinking nervously as if she needed shielding. She was small, her chin-length hair straight and plain, with ebony strands that now blew in the slight breeze.

She's awful damn pretty. The errant thought came to Rusty out of nowhere, as did images he hadn't replayed in years. He remembered big, frightened green eyes that seemed to see everything, and ragged-cut hair, dark and tattered as old black silk. He remembered her forlorn expression.

He didn't remember pretty.

"Oh, I didn't see you there," she said, and twisted to face him.

Her hands clutched the car's streamlined window frame and he noticed she wore a severe gray suit with heels. Her body was slim, with every curve a man liked to see. Little Lucy had become a woman.

"Uh," she said, "it *has* been a long time. Fifteen years since I've been here."

"Since the divorce," Rusty said, dismounting. "Our parents must have had the shortest marriage on record." Six months, to be exact, Rusty remembered silently, before Lucy's mother decided she didn't like country living—and didn't like the rancher with whom she'd exchanged vows. She'd packed up her car, her annoying little lap dog and Lucy.

"How is your mother?" he asked. Best to get the formalities over with.

"Living abroad," she answered curtly. "Remarried. A shipping magnate this time, I think."

"You don't talk to her much, then?"

She shrugged, but under her calm, he could feel her emotions. Lucy and her mom weren't cut from the same cloth; he knew that from way back.

Not that it mattered to him. None of his business.

He saw her glance over the sprawling two-story house, the white-painted outbuildings of barns, sheds and bunkhouse. His gaze followed hers, seeing what she saw, and he winced. How evident was the peeling paint? How obvious the overgrown weeds, the half-broken fence posts?

"It's the same," she whispered, though her words drifted to him on the cold breeze. "Nothing's changed. Nothing."

"That bad, huh?" His jaw clenched.

"No." For the first time she fixed her gaze fully on his. "It's wonderful. I feel like...like I'm home."

The direct impact of her emerald eyes hit him with far more force than was right. A memory of the tiny urchin she'd been, crouched in the old oak tree in the meadow, came streaming into his consciousness. At fifteen, he'd been more concerned with his horses, his friends and the sassy neighbor girl than the mousy kid his new stepmother had brought to the ranch.

Up in the oak, Lucy had been crying; Rusty had seen the tear tracks on her pale cheeks. He'd tried to coax her down, but she'd shaken her head.

So he'd climbed.

Since he'd already learned she spoke in nothing but monosyllables, he didn't question her. They merely sat together, a fifteen-year-old boy and a ten-year-old girl, watching the sun cast swaths of amber and gold over the cottonwoods in the meadow. They probably clung to that big branch together for an hour, wordless, until darkness transformed the sun's golden streaks to cobalt and then to black.

When the first stars winked into existence she let him help her down. He put her behind his saddle and rode with her to the house. On the ground, she'd looked up at him with those incredible eyes and he'd seen her chin tremble. He'd smiled at her and tousled her hair. She'd given him a shy, tremulous smile in return. It was the first and only expression of happiness he'd ever seen in her, a spark of joy in an otherwise wan countenance.

Now Rusty shook his head, impatient again, but this time with himself. He had no time for reminiscing.

"Come to the house," he said more abruptly than he'd meant to. "Fritzy can make coffee." Fritzy—the family's always-smiling housekeeper—had been with the Sheffields for twenty years.

He called out, and a youth appeared from the barn to take his horse. Down at the branding chutes, men were working cattle, roping them one by one and applying the hot Lazy S brand. Turning back to Lucy, he asked, "You want to stay the night, don't you? I expect it's too far to drive back. Got any luggage?"

Taking careful steps in her heeled shoes, she came out from her hiding place and opened the trunk. "Yes, it's here."

Bending down, she went to grasp her tweed suitcase when he quickly reached out, saying, "I'll get it," and bumped her shoulder.

She gasped—a startled big-eyed doe.

Rusty frowned, wondering what had gotten into her. Why was she so skittish? After all, he was the one with the right to be nervous, not her. She was going to get what she wanted. He would be the loser.

Still, he didn't like the way she flinched from him, as if he'd done something wrong or was contemplating it. The idea offended him; he'd never harmed a woman in his life or even wanted to.

He must have scowled because she mumbled, "Sorry."

"No apology needed." Shaking his head, he hefted her large suitcase from the trunk.

"Thank you," she said in a voice so low it was nearly a whisper. Her slim fingers curled beneath her chin now, her eyes lowered to screen her expression. But the flash of what he'd seen there disturbed him. Rusty didn't know what turns her life had taken, but one thing was certain. Lucy Donovan hid many secrets.

Lucy trailed Rusty Sheffield into the house, berating herself for jumping like a frightened rabbit when he'd only wanted to help her carry the suitcase.

But she didn't like men who took over a situation like they'd been voted boss. She was uncomfortable around aggressive, overtly masculine men.

Somehow she hadn't been prepared for the incredibly handsome, overwhelming *maleness* Rusty exuded. Formerly auburn, his hair had darkened nearly to brown. At least, she thought so from what she could see of it under his hat. No longer a gawky youth, the man had grown to over six feet tall. Beneath his yoked Western shirt his chest was brawny, his arms, revealed by his rolled-up sleeves, were thick with muscle. His thighs were powerful, his waist narrow. He even smelled good, like fresh-turned earth and high-mountain winds.

Oh, she noticed everything about him, cataloged the changes that maturation had wrought. And it seemed to Lucy that everything about him was too much. He was too big, too observant, too handsome, too…well, *manly*.

Rusty Sheffield made her edgy.

She wished she were completely composed, a woman with confidence and style and sophistication. But miserably she knew she'd never done anything meaningful in her life. The counselor she'd seen had told her that confidence was developed when someone worked hard at a task or skill and became proficient at it. She had recommended Lucy learn a profession, or go to college and earn a degree, perhaps start a business.

Coward that she was, she'd done nothing of the kind.

Still, she did have one goal. A goal that for once she intended to reach.

If only she weren't so anxious.

"This way," Rusty instructed, preceding her through the front door of the wood-sided house. The screen frame banged behind her in exactly the same way it had fifteen years ago. She smiled.

Inside, the house had experienced few changes, as well. The old davenport with its cabbage-rose print still reigned as the centerpiece of the large living area. It was flanked by antique tea carts with Tiffany lamps and faced by several oversized leather chairs. Gray river rock lovingly laid fifty years before formed the fireplace with its mantel, which held a collection of figurines. Against the wall a hall tree held coiled lariats, and at the bottom, neat rows of cowboy boots lined up like soldiers waiting to be called to service.

In the kitchen across the hallway, Lucy heard someone stirring, probably Fritzy. The smell of freshly baked bread wafted to her.

More pleased than she could say, Lucy sighed, but Rusty set her suitcase down and walked straight through to the small office his father had formerly occupied. She guessed the room was Rusty's now.

"Sit down." He pointed to a striped seat opposite, throwing himself into a castered chair to regard her levelly across the desktop. Behind him bookshelves rose to the ceiling, and the file cabinet beside his desk had papers overflowing the drawers. The room gave her the impression of ordered chaos. He said, "I want to get this over with as soon as possible."

She lowered herself into the striped chair, but found she couldn't relax enough to rest her spine against its back.

"Over the telephone, you said you had money," he began bluntly, and she forced herself not to wince. "What is it you want, exactly?"

Lucy drew a deep, deep breath. If ever she needed courage, it was now. *Please,* she prayed to the Powers Above, *please let my dream come true.* Lacing her fingers together in her lap, she plunged in. "As you know, I've heard about the death of your brothers. The news traveled fast. I'm so sorry. The accident was a terrible tragedy."

Stone-faced, he gave only a curt nod.

The head-on collision between his brother Landon's pickup and an eighteen-wheeler had made sad, local headlines. A freak accident, both Landon and his other brother, Tom, had died instantly, as had the other driver. Folks said the resulting fiery explosion had echoed for miles. Investigating authorities never discovered what made Landon's truck cross the center divider. Authorities guessed he'd been reaching for one of his ever-present cigarettes. Or possibly stretching down to the cell phone kept on the floor between the two seats.

Lucy hadn't met Tom or Landon. The boys were away during her short stay at the ranch. But she knew they'd been well liked.

"As a result, you now hold full title to the Lazy S, right?" She glanced around the room. "I don't suppose you ever expected to, with two older brothers who would have had first claim here."

He hesitated. "No."

"Rusty, I told you when I called I have money, and it's true. My life hasn't been terribly…eventful," she said, awkward yet determined to get through this, "but I did get married."

She saw his eyebrows arch, though she didn't blame him for his surprise. She wasn't any great catch. At least that's what Kenneth had always enjoyed saying.

"Well, a year ago, my husband passed away—" she forced herself to stare Rusty straight in the eyes "—leaving me a wealthy widow."

His gaze drifted away and his expression became thoughtful. Rubbing his chin, he said, "I see."

Probably not. He probably saw only what he wanted to, but she needed to press on. With uncharacteristic boldness, she blurted, "I want to purchase the Lazy S."

"*Purchase it?*" He stared at her. "The whole place?" His pitying glance raked her. "I thought maybe you just wanted to lease a couple of acres, maybe run a few horses or build a cabin. The Lazy S comprises several thousand acres of prime grazing land. We have water rights to the creek, twelve hundred head of mother cows and as many calves, a hundred and fifty horses and dozens of blooded bulls. The property alone is worth a small fortune.''

Casually he tossed out a figure, let it hover in the air between them like an alien spacecraft.

Lucy did not blink.

He studied her face. After a moment, disbelief gave way to dawning awareness. ''You've got that much?''

Again, she merely kept her gaze steady and waited for him to draw his own conclusions. The spacecraft vanished, left only the trailing vapor of Rusty's incredulity.

Taking off his hat, he stabbed stiff fingers through his thick hair. It *was* brown, as she'd thought, the deep rich color of brewed coffee. After a moment he let out a long, slow breath. She could feel his shock and sense his struggle to assimilate her changed status in life.

Lounging back in his chair, he stacked his booted feet atop a low file cabinet. ''Well, that's something. Lucy, I guess you've done all right for yourself.''

''It wasn't me,'' she corrected him quickly. ''I didn't do anything to earn it. It was my husband's—his commercial real estate business.''

''But it's yours now.''

''Yes.'' She shifted uncomfortably. ''But I didn't— that is—'' She caught herself. It was not part of her plan to explain every single thing to him. She cleared her throat. ''Well, will you sell?''

Dropping his boots to the wooden floor with a thud, he got abruptly to his feet. He snatched up his hat, jammed it on his head and pulled it low across his eyes. With his big palms splayed over the desk, he leaned toward her. ''Not if you had ten million, Lucy. Not twenty. Maybe from your rich sugar daddy you learned you can buy most things. But not everything. Not the

Lazy S." Straightening, he took swift strides away from her. "Thanks for coming. You probably won't want to spend the night after all. It was...interesting seeing you again."

"Wait," she cried. Now she'd gone and done it. She'd insulted his masculine pride. "I didn't mean to offend you." But he was already pacing through the living room toward the front door. Hurrying after him, she caught her foot on a table leg and stumbled, nearly falling. He didn't turn.

"Rusty," she said, "I'm not trying to put you out of your family home."

At the front door Rusty kept walking. "Sure sounds like it."

Outside, afternoon sunlight momentarily blinded her, though the bright rays offered no warmth. Cold fall air bit at her exposed throat, numbed her fingers. "No...you don't understand." He was halfway to the barn. "Stop, Rusty, please," she said again. "There's more. I don't want you to leave the ranch. I want you to stay on."

In the shadows of the great barn, he slowed. He turned to face her, hands on hips. "Beg pardon?"

Reaching him, she knew she was wringing her hands but was powerless to stop. "I know about your financial troubles, Rusty. I know that before their deaths your brothers heavily mortgaged this place. Your law career in San Francisco was successful and you've made a good living, but it's not enough to put the ranch in the black."

His face hardened. "How do you know all that?"

Apologetically she said, "I've got my own lawyers. You know they can find out anything."

With a snort he pivoted and disappeared into the barn.

She followed. Coming out of direct sunlight, she found it dark inside, and for a moment could hardly see. The air was cooler and full of the smell of alfalfa hay and animals. She wrapped her arms about her middle and suppressed a shiver. Long banks of stalls with horses inside, a tack room that held halters and bridles and work saddles and a grooming area took up the big barn.

She found him pulling on heavy work gloves and standing beside stacks of baled hay. "I'll pay whatever price you ask, Rusty. I need the ranch. I...I need you."

At this last he paused and gave her a slow up-and-down perusal. "For what, Lucy?" he asked in a dangerously quiet voice. "What do you need me for?"

Groping for courage, she deliberately stiffened her spine. "To manage the property, of course. To direct employees, make business decisions, buy livestock—I don't know. For all of what's needed. I...I don't know the first thing about running a cattle ranch."

He glanced derisively at her sling-backed pumps. "No kidding."

Shivers began to tremble through her. She couldn't back down now; he had to be made to understand. "I don't know much about ranching, Rusty. But I do know one thing. The time I spent here was the best of my life. I *need* this place." She gestured around. "It sounds crazy, but...I need that big old friendly ranch house. I need the smell of horses, hot from a run. I need familiar people around me. I...need the oak tree in the meadow."

As he looked into her eyes she wondered if he understood her. She wondered if he remembered their afternoon in the tree together—that day so long ago when she'd been weeping because her mother had declared that she found horses boring and cattle smelly. She was getting a divorce as soon as she could hunt down an attorney. She was bored, bored, bored—not least of all with her husband, Howard Sheffield, the "unsophisticated, countrified bumpkin" she had married in a temporary fit of Las Vegas-inspired insanity.

"We'll be leaving the Lazy S," Lucy's mother had announced to her, "first thing in the morning!"

The memory sprang alive in Lucy's mind, of her heartache and then of seeking solace high up in the tree, its shielding branches her only comfort. The scene was so tangible in her mind she fancied she could almost reach out and touch that sunset's glorious golden colors. Almost touch the kind boy Rusty Sheffield had been.

She had to keep going forward, stop reliving the past. "I-I've got an idea, Rusty, of what we might do here. We could bring in people who want a taste of country life—stressed-out people from the city. They could put on jeans and ride and help move cattle." As a child she had gained so much here; was it any wonder she wished others to experience the same happiness? "I figure they could stay for a week or two," she went on with growing enthusiasm, "enjoy this marvelous place. See what it's like to—"

"A *dude ranch?*" He cut through her ardent stream with a disbelieving guffaw. "You mean to turn the Lazy S into a greenhorn hotel?"

"Well, call it what you will." She shrugged, trying not to be put off by his discouraging tone. Once she could fully explain, fully define the entire scope of her vision, he would comprehend everything. "I've put a lot of thought into this, worked out the details in my mind. I realize the notion is new to you, Rusty, and you need time to digest everything, but it could be like a...a health ranch. We could put in a swimming pool, have yoga classes—"

"No half-dressed yogi is gonna run around here spouting New-Age manure." His expression closed her off like the slamming of a door. "We don't need any damn pool, either. We're simple folk. If we get hot, we just jump in the creek." Features stiff, he collected a pair of hay hooks and thrust them into a thick bale. For a disturbing instant she had the crazy notion he'd like to use the hay hooks on her.

To heft the heavy bale into a wheelbarrow, he braced his feet. "I don't know how I'll get out from under this financial mess, but I won't sell the Lazy S. And it won't *ever* become a dude ranch."

But why not? she wondered, blinking at him.

Recognizing a brick wall when she slammed into one, Lucy felt fingers of despair reaching into her heart like tendrils of mist before an ominous fog. Her attorneys had been so sure Rusty would jump at the chance to avoid certain bankruptcy that she had counted on his agreement. And the lawyers, the accountants and the bank officials had all concurred: without her, he *would* go bankrupt.

Staring sightlessly at her hands, she supposed she could wait for the foreclosure and simply buy the property from the bank. But that wasn't how she wanted it. She wanted the Lazy S *and* Rusty. If only as a business partner.

Deep inside her soul, a silent bell of loneliness and pain began its familiar, dismal peal. All her life, she'd quit everything she'd started, given in when she should

have fought back, accepted "no" when she should
have demanded "yes." The lonely, pealing toll grew
in her mind until she could almost feel its grim vibra-
tions.

Not this time. She crushed the defeating voice inside.
This time I'll stand firm. She swore to it.

"You're part of the deal," she whispered to his
back, her throat tight and aching. "Don't you see? You
complete everything."

His biceps straining, Rusty lifted the bale into the
wheelbarrow and rolled it to the bank of stalls, broke
it open and methodically tossed six-inch thick flakes
into feeder bins. In the end stall, a hungry buckskin
mare whinnied. Rusty didn't look up at Lucy. "What
sort of man was he?"

She blinked. "Who?"

"Your husband, Lucy. Was he good to you?"

The unexpected question blindsided her. She
couldn't think of a thing to say.

"That's not too personal a question to ask, is it? Was
your husband—what was his name?"

"Kenneth."

"Kenneth, then." He tossed a chunky flake into the
next stall. "Was Kenneth a man who treated his
woman well? Were you happy with him?"

"I...I don't, that is—" She licked her lips, took a
deep breath and tried again. "Kenneth had many fine
qualities."

The narrow-eyed glance he shot over his shoulder
sliced straight through her like a shard of broken glass.
When they were younger, most of the time he'd barely
noticed her. But on the infrequent occasions when he
had, she well recalled his piercing, perceptive eyes. Al-

ways he'd appeared able to read her innermost thoughts.

Lucy swallowed and forced her mind back to business. "The ranch, Rusty. If you won't let me help, how can you keep it? Who else could you turn to?"

As he faced her, finished with the afternoon feeding, she saw that his skin was drawn taut over his cheekbones; his brown eyes took on a hard glitter. Tension radiated from every line in his body, and she felt his frustration beating at her in waves. Jerkily he stripped off his gloves.

For a moment he stared at the ground. It was a strangely dejected look for such a confident, strong man. She wondered at it. At last he raised his head.

"Sell you half," he ground out.

"What?" Lucy stared at him dumbly.

"I'll sell you half interest. God knows it's the last thing I want. I thought I could raise capital selling you a few acres. But you want it all, don't you?" His eyes narrowed. "And you're right. There's little choice. The bank's gonna take it if I don't act. I can't believe it, but you're my best—and only—option."

Wisely she refrained from telling him she knew this.

"I get full control over the running of the ranch," he demanded. "You'll be a partner, but mostly in name and on paper."

Pulse beating wildly, she said, "What about my idea—opening the ranch to others?" She didn't dare use the term he found so derisive.

"We'll work that out," he evaded. "And no promises. Meantime, the property will be appraised, and you'll invest exactly half the amount right back here."

"Certainly," she said.

"And you understand that I have final say in everything pertaining to ranch business, at least for this year?''

''Sure, but—''

''One more thing. If I can raise the same amount you're investing, I have the right to buy you out. Agreed?''

Lucy faltered. That wasn't what she wanted at all. When he got enough money he'd simply throw her off the ranch?

He continued staring at her in his hard-eyed way.

The capital she'd agreed to invest was quite a healthy sum. Would he be able to raise it…ever? It seemed unlikely. Besides, if he could, by then he'd have gotten to know her better, maybe even grown fond of her. By then, perhaps she'd have carved out a place for herself on the Lazy S. It seemed an unlikely event.

''You get a year,'' she said, thinking fast.

He looked stunned. ''What?''

''If you can raise the money in one year's time, I'll agree to it.'' Behind her back, she twisted her chilled fingers together, hoping against hope he'd settle on this. ''And, I get my dude ranch. On that point you have to agree.'' There, she'd said it.

Rusty's mouth flattened. He squeezed his eyes shut and muttered a word she pretended not to hear. ''Fine,'' he spat out. ''A year it is. And in running things here, you won't interfere?''

''No.'' A welling joy rose in her chest like champagne bubbles. She wanted to shout her delight to the world. She wanted to sing. She wanted to rush to Rusty and throw her arms around him.

''My word's as good as a contract,'' he informed

her coolly, and instead of the hug she would prefer, he proffered a broad palm.

"Thank you," she said, smiling tremulously. Enclosing his hand in both her own, she shook it warmly. "Thank you."

What the hell had he done, Rusty asked himself an hour later as he walked to the corrals. Just what? The situation was impossible. Had he really agreed to sell his former stepsister half the ranch? And how were they supposed to live—together in the big house—a bachelor and a young widow woman?

Fighting down resentment, he watched her walk to her zippy, completely impractical sports car and retrieve a purse and a shoulder bag. Her body beneath the plain gray suit was compact, her derriere firm. Though not large, her breasts appeared well rounded.

Rummaging in the back seat, Lucy bent at the waist. The action hiked her skirt up several inches above her knees and presented him with a view of slim, smooth-skinned thighs. Outlined by the gray fabric, her rump curved sweetly: taut, yet rounded just right. He wondered how she'd look without the ugly suit. An image of a nude Lucy reclining on the navy sheets of his bed instantly flooded his mind. He found it alarmingly arousing.

Grimacing, he turned to go check on the automatic waterers. Great. Alone together in the house with an all-grown-up Lucy, and him already picturing her firm body unclothed and splayed on his bed like a centerfold.

It was crazy. He didn't even like her. At least, he disliked what she'd forced him to do. Hated it, actually. His hands fisted.

Fortunately Fritzy was staying in the house and not in her cottage. She seemed happy living there; he didn't think she'd mind staying on.

He entered his gelding's stall and went to the waterer in back. The horse raised its head a brief moment from its dinner, chewing. Its dark eyes asked ancient questions.

What did Lucy want, really? Not for a minute did he believe that business about her needing the damn house and horsey smells. It was odd, though, the way she'd shied away earlier when he'd only bumped her arm. And how evasive she'd been when he asked about her husband.

Somehow he'd get the cash to buy her out. He'd work night and day, save everything. There were many ways other than raising cattle to make money on a ranch, especially one with the rich resources of the Lazy S. Ways his brothers hadn't even begun to explore. He would tap them all.

Her ludicrous proposal of turning the ranch into a vacation spot rankled. He vowed that the public hordes would come trampling onto the Lazy S only over his dead, decomposing body. A years-old scene came vividly to his mind: his father addressing him and his brothers, each word ringing with clarity.

"We must keep the land pure," Howard Sheffield had exhorted his three almost-grown sons. "I won't be around forever, and the ranch'll pass to you, just as it did to me and my brother from our daddy."

The three teenagers sat at attention in their father's office and listened solemnly.

"You boys have to carry on the family tradition. It'll be hard, I know, to resist commercialism, and this new business of catering to city slickers so many of our friends have succumbed to. It brings in money, but, by God, there's got to be other ways.''

To Rusty's seventeen-year-old eyes, his father suddenly looked old—Howard's sun-roughened skin was splotched with benign cancers, his eyes rheumy. For Rusty it was a small shock, yet it came abruptly. His father was the burly, iron-willed constant on the ranch, the immortal bulwark for them all against a cruel world.

However, in that instant Rusty knew the first glimmerings of maturing youth: his father wouldn't always be there to solve problems, to repair their mistakes made from inexperience. Someday, maybe soon, he'd have to grow up, take on full adult responsibilities.

"Dad," he said, anxious and uncomfortable with his thoughts, "don't worry. We're not gonna let a bunch of strangers overrun the ranch.''

Howard fixed his youngest with a particularly penetrating stare. "See that you don't. Jim Curlan'd give ten years off his life if he could get rid of his sideline. So'd old Harley Jacobson down at the Flying J. They need the money, I can understand that. God knows there's more lean years than fat ones running a ranch. But as a result their spreads have been spoiled. All those damned idiots from the city playing cowboy, ruining good horses, getting underfoot, pistol-shootin' at anything that flies by.'' He snorted, then paused to look thoughtfully at each of his sons.

"Now, boys, promise me you'll never sell out. Keep the Lazy S as it's always been. In the family. Swear it.''

The memory receded on Howard's binding dictum and the grave vow Rusty and his brothers had made.

The fact that the other two had passed away now, leaving only Rusty to uphold the promise was entirely irrelevant. He'd given his word, and failure was unacceptable.

At the end of this year he would exercise the clause he'd write into his contract with Lucy. She would be gone. It would just take time, he knew that. From the training in his former career as a contracts attorney working for major corporate accounts, he would have no trouble wording their agreement into cast-iron legal language. Every clause would be phrased to favor him—and not Lucy Donovan.

The gelding moved to nuzzle his shoulder. The waterer was working fine. Absently he rubbed the horse's withers. Something was wrong in Lucy's life. Something…

Again the image of her jerking away from him came back and suddenly he knew. Thinking of it, he closed his eyes and wondered how he hadn't realized it before.

Lucy had come to the Lazy S to heal.

He hadn't told her everything. Wait until she found out that the ranch she'd just purchased half interest in came with an added bonus. Suddenly he grinned. What would she say when he presented her with a pink-skinned, milk-swilling, diaper-wetting, loudly squalling six-month-old baby?

Chapter Two

The ear-splitting squawk behind Lucy startled her so badly she whirled. Her purse and briefcase flew from her hands, skittered across the living room's floor and slammed into the cabbage-rose-print davenport. Lipstick, keys and a checkbook hurled from the purse while file folders and assorted legal papers spewed from the briefcase.

Fritzy stood in the kitchen doorway. Her eyebrows were raised, but she was smiling. However it wasn't the older woman with whom Lucy had enjoyed a reunion an hour ago that had startled her, but the grinning, drooling, chortling creature Fritzy held in her arms.

A baby. Fritzy was holding a baby.

"Sorry we scared you," Fritzy said, the apology much too offhand for Lucy's still-pounding heart, "but Baby sure does like squealin'."

Lucy laid a hand on her chest. "So I gather. Whose,

um...baby is it?'' Shakily she bent to stuff papers into the briefcase.

"Oh, didn't Rusty tell you before he went back to branding?''

It was true that less than an hour ago Rusty had informed her tersely that he was ''burning daylight'' and stomped off toward the corrals.

The housekeeper went on airily. ''The men've got to get those late calves marked before cold weather sets in and then moved to low pastures. Fall roundup's not so important as spring, but—''

"Uh, Fritzy,'' Lucy gently reminded her, ''the baby?''

"Oh, this is Tom's. You remember, one of Rusty's brothers?'' The graying woman shook her head sadly. "Such a shame, him dallying with that gal. Even *she* said it was just one night—but when will people learn—that's all it takes!''

The baby waved plump arms and flexed its feet, forcing Fritzy to shift the weight to one generous hip. Her soft-printed house dress bunched up a little, but Fritzy didn't appear to notice. The infant's blue eyes stared back at Lucy, and she noticed the rounded head was bald but for a soft bit of auburn down. The child's body was stuffed like a sausage into a pink terry one-piece suit, the seams pulled so tight Lucy could see frayed threads threatening to burst. She shrugged; maybe that's how baby clothes were supposed to fit. On the creature's feet were a kind of bootie, white, with mock laces.

The tot squealed again.

"Fritzy, what do you mean it's Tom's?'' Lucy asked warily. She straightened to place her purse and case onto the couch. She'd never had any experience with children. In the first months of her marriage, Kenneth had gone off without her knowledge and paid a surgeon to perform a vasectomy. Kids got in the way, he'd said. Kids were a nuisance. Kids were a pain in the a—

"Tom got that woman pregnant, like I said," Fritzy supplied. "Then that freeway accident happened and...well, after she delivered, she showed up here, shoved Baby at Rusty and said, 'You keep the brat, I don't want her.'" Fritzy harrumphed and nuzzled the infant's neck. "Imagine, abandoning a child just like that. It's terrible. But we don't mind, do we, Baby?" She finished by making a silly face at the child.

Before Lucy could voice another question, Fritzy glanced up. "You'll help, won't you dear? Not that I wouldn't love to spend every minute with such a perfect little lamb, but I've got housekeeping to do, you know." Without waiting for a reply, she came forward and bundled the baby into Lucy's arms. "Hold my angel a bit. I've got to get that chicken roasting or we'll have no supper!"

"No, wait!" Lucy cried as a warm sloppy mouth came flush with her throat, depositing spittle down her neck, and a wriggling body smashed against her chest. "Fritzy," she wailed at the woman's fast-retreating back, "I don't know how—I can't do this."

"Nothing to it," the housekeeper said with a wave of her hand.

Lucy dashed after her, awkwardly balancing the child in her arms. In the spacious kitchen with its sunflower yellow curtains and cozy nook, Fritzy lifted a large blue-speckled roasting pan onto the tiled countertop and settled a raw chicken into its depths.

"Just a minute," Lucy panted. Babies were heavier than she would have guessed they could be. "I've got to get this straight. Are you saying that Rusty's brother Tom indulged in a one-night stand with some woman he didn't know, and that this baby was born after his death?''

"Yes, dear." Without looking up, Fritzy began spreading the chicken skin with herbs, then shook salt and pepper on top.

"And then," Lucy continued doggedly, determined to get matters clear, "the woman came here and sort of...dropped it off?" On her shoulder, tiny fingers tried to pull one of Lucy's small hoop earrings into its mouth. Lucy batted at the pudgy, grabbing hands. She was beginning to have a terrible sinking sensation in the pit of her stomach.

"Yes, dear." Fritzy poured a cup of what looked like broth into the roaster and took up a basting brush to paint melted butter over the chicken.

"*Ouch,*" Lucy yelped. The child had clamped the earring and her earlobe into its fist and was pulling both toward the yawing maw of its mouth. Dismayed, Lucy wondered how such a minuscule hand could wield all the strength of a lumberjack. With great difficulty, considering she had to juggle the infant with one arm, she finally managed to free her ear.

Over her shoulder Fritzy smiled. "You shouldn't wear jewelry any more," she said. "At least not for a while. Babies are like crows—everything that glitters catches their eyes." She chuckled at her own joke.

Lucy did not laugh. The sinking sensation had reached her toes. "You can't mean," she began, speaking slowly and distinctly so that Fritzy wouldn't misunderstand, "that this baby lives *here,* in this house."

The housekeeper paused in surprise. She smoothed her gingham apron over her stout midsection. "Course

I do. Gracious, where would you expect the child to live? It's why I moved up from my cottage. I was thinking of moving back sometime, but,'' she frowned, then resumed her work, "I s'pose with you here now I'd best stay. Wouldn't be right—an eligible bachelor like Rusty and a sweet young thing like you living alone under one roof.'' Her graying topknot bobbled as she shook her head. "No, indeed.''

Of all the developments Lucy had expected to arise from her business deal with Rusty, she'd never considered anything like this. Numbed by shock, she wondered what other little surprises Rusty might have in store for her.

Lucy placed her protesting burden in the crib while she took three minutes to change into her jeans, an old black sweatshirt and tennis shoes, and twenty more to wrestle the baby's flailing, stubby limbs into a new diaper and another too-tight suit. Fritzy insisted she had kitchen work, that Lucy could *of course* change Baby—there was *nothing* to it—and had sent her off with a box of diapers.

The child's bedroom was on the second floor, between the one Rusty had assigned to her and his own. A wood-slatted crib with clown-print bedding, a lamp and a changing table were the only pieces of furniture. The walls were an unadorned white, and nothing much matched. Even to Lucy's untrained eye, the nursery appeared bare. Weren't there supposed to be teddy bears, toy chests, hanging colored mobiles?

At the changing table, the disposable hourglass-shaped diaper was fitted with confusing tapes, which maddeningly kept sticking to her skin, to the bedding and even together. Then Lucy somehow got the baby's arms into the outfit's leg holes and the legs into the arm holes before she managed to figure out the intricacies of such an ensemble, but in the end she was triumphant.

And she learned that the child was a girl.

Lucy blew a strand of hair from her eyes.

Presumably to show gratitude, the baby squealed with impressive volume.

"You're welcome," Lucy replied. Guessing the pink plastic pail beside the changing table was the dirty diaper receptacle, she bent low and removed the tight-fitting top. Like demons from Pandora's box, an eye-watering, brain-numbing odor of revoltingly appalling proportions burst forth.

Lucy staggered, slammed down the lid and abandoned the diaper on the table for Fritzy to deal with later. In the hallway she paused and took grateful moments to breathe in lungfuls of clean air.

Back in the kitchen with her cleaned-up human cargo, Lucy expected Fritzy to be suitably impressed and ready to take over, but the corpulent woman, now peeling potatoes, merely suggested she carry the child down to the corrals.

"Fritzy," Lucy said carefully, still holding the infant, "I, uh, don't know how to do stuff with a baby."

"Stuff?"

"You know…things." Trying to explain, Lucy floundered while the baby attempted to flop out of her arms. She struggled to hold the slippery infant. "Like…feed her. Or, um, give her a bath. Or—" What else *did* one do with babies? "Uh, or other stuff."

"Lucy, Lucy," Fritzy replied kindly, "don't worry. You'll learn. Experience is the best teacher."

"I'm afraid," Lucy explained even more kindly,

"that this will have to remain your job. I'm not very maternal." Hadn't Kenneth told her many times that she'd make a poor mother?

Because she knew she and her husband would never become parents, she'd long avoided children, ignored baby shower invitations, declined to hold acquaintances' newborns. Why should she, when she'd never get one of her own—when cuddling someone else's darling only made the ache for her own children sting so profoundly?

She tried to hand over the child, but Fritzy scoffed, peeling another potato.

"It'll be all right, Lucy, you'll see. Now, why don't you go down to the corrals? Baby just loves to see the horses." She turned her back and filled an enormous pot with water, salted it, and then began slicing potatoes inside.

Alarm replaced Lucy's growing apprehension, spiked up her spine like a hand running over barbwire. Fritzy was determined that Lucy help in child care, of this she had no further illusions. Slice went Fritzy's paring knife, plop went the potato into the water. Frustrated, Lucy stared at Fritzy's broad back.

Fritzy ignored her.

Slice. Plop. Slice. Plop.

This was ridiculous. How dare Rusty neglect to mention this almost-brand-new child to her!

She'd come to the Lazy S searching for peace, for quiet and tranquility.

Not squalling voices and grabby fingers and...peepee!

"I will go down to the corrals," she said aloud. If Fritzy was going to be stubborn, she'd get Rusty to take the child. It was his niece, wasn't it? "Nothing

personal," she whispered into the baby's shell-like ear.
Suddenly she noticed that the baby's scent was different from anything she'd ever smelled before. Different but good, and thank goodness nothing like that disgusting diaper pail. No, more like fresh-from-the-oven buns or soft, lovable puppies.

She shook off the thought. "I'm just not the motherly sort," she whispered. "You understand, don't you?"

Baby cooed.

With a fleecy blanket Fritzy handed her, Lucy managed to wrap the child up against the cooling air, clamp it to her chest and march out.

Autumn was beginning to cloak western Nevada in hues of russet and claret, turning the leaves of grouped alder and spruce trees into a fall-colored kaleidoscope. Winter sun had nearly sunk behind the fanged upthrust of the Humboldt mountains.

Outside the house, Lucy paused a moment to draw a breath. Pure, lung-expanding air filled her chest, scented of sage and the faintest hint of a branding fire. For once, the tyke made no sound, merely nestled her face into the crook of Lucy's neck. The sensation wasn't so bad, she thought, not really minding the child's wet mouth anymore. And she so enjoyed the chirrup of the coming night crickets and the breeze soughing serenely through the trees' brittle leaves.

There was no honking of angry commuters, no blare of city sirens, no suffocating exhaust fumes. One could relax here, find solace from the frenetic pace of city life.

These qualities were why she'd come to the country, she thought, pleased. Others should have the chance to enjoy this wonderful environment. How easily she could picture groups of twenty or so—nice, hardworking city folk who needed a place to relax, appreciate country sunshine, wildlife, the great outdoors.

As a child, her short time here had bolstered her for the hard years to come. Always when life mired her in difficulty, she could close her eyes and travel in her mind to the ranch and find relief.

Rusty could be persuaded to see her side, surely he could. He was set in his ways and proud, she could see that. She would just have to explain matters more thoroughly.

But he couldn't be allowed to get away with his deception about the child. With determined strides, she crunched her way over the gravel-lined drive to the corrals, where at least eight men appeared to be just finishing their work.

At the far end of the large enclosure, a man worked, mounted on a deep-brass-colored horse. Why Lucy's eyes should focus so swiftly on Rusty she didn't know—but she didn't even have to look for him. He was dressed the same as, and he worked the same as, the cowboys inside. Yet the unique tilt of his black Stetson and the confident set of his broad shoulders somehow set him apart from other men.

Across the corral Rusty concentrated on swinging his rope overhead. He took his aim, made his throw and captured the first of two hefty remaining calves. Then he dragged the animal to the men waiting at the branding fire. He was bone weary from the full day's work and the unsettling meeting with his former stepsister. It wasn't every day a man had to sell off half his heritage. He grimaced.

When the men were finished, they released the calf,

which lurched to its feet and trotted over to its bawling mother. The mama cow sniffed her calf, determined it was fine and wandered off, trailing the reassured young animal.

Still on horseback, Rusty caught sight of Lucy and signaled for one of the others to rope the last calf. He coiled his rope and guided his horse to where she stood holding Baby, on the other side of the rail fence.

Drawing rein before her, he leaned one forearm on the horn and the other atop that. Nudging back his hat with a thumb, he observed, "I see you've made Baby's acquaintance."

"I certainly have," she acknowledged, a tart hint of warning in her voice.

She was so pretty, he admitted for the second time that day. Her jet hair blew attractively across her face and the skin of her cheeks and lips had pinkened in the crisp fall air. Another man, one who might be interested in pursuing a woman like Lucy, would definitely think her lips kissable. If she thought her oversized sweatshirt was hiding the thrust of her breasts, she was mistaken. And her slim thighs and hips were damn near hugged by her snug jeans.

Stiffly he straightened in the saddle. It was a good thing *he* wasn't interested in her. He was her reluctant business partner, and she was someone who would find herself tossed off the Lazy S in twelve short months.

"She's quite a little surprise," Lucy went on. "I wonder how it is that you didn't mention her before." She waited, eyeing him steadily and not, he thought, with an approving expression.

He grinned, enjoying her discomfort. "Aw, you'll get used to her. We're all crazy about Baby around here.'' He guessed he'd have to start some sort of adoption proceedings soon, make things legal.

As she juggled the squirming child with inept hands, Rusty's grin widened. She'd been married, but obviously didn't have any kids. Hadn't she ever coped with a six-month old?

She glared at him over the top of the auburn head, her annoyance palpable in the air between them. ''You might have told me.''

''Why?'' He shrugged. ''You were so anxious to buy into the place— Well, Baby comes along with it.'' He leaned forward, saddle creaking, and murmured to the child in cutesy tones he hoped would irritate Lucy.

Hearing his familiar voice, Baby gurgled happily, and when Rusty's sorrel gelding snuffled her head, she launched into a bout of giggles that ended in hiccups.

Lucy had her arms full, and by her awkwardness, Rusty's original thought was confirmed: it was plain as the whiskers on his gelding's nose that the woman had no experience at all with children.

Baby jounced happily, banging the top of her head against Lucy's chin. Lucy freed a hand to rub her jaw, her scowl at Rusty intensifying.

He tried not to laugh. It served her right, forcing him to sell her half the Lazy S as she'd done. Too bad it wouldn't do her much good. In twelve months' time, he'd have the money—no question about it. And fetching as Lucy was, she would not be allowed to dissuade him.

Myriad fund-raising ideas filled his head; tonight he'd make calls and see if he could sell gypsum, a produce used for insulation, plaster and wallboard, from a pit on the farthest reaches of the property. His brothers had always resisted mining on the Lazy S, but

Rusty knew they'd made poor decisions. He realized, grimly and with some pain, that he could no longer afford to stand on principles.

The baby jounced again and Lucy nearly dropped her. At last Rusty took pity. "Take Baby back to the house. Fritzy can handle her."

Instantly he knew his phrasing had been poor. Over the baby's head Lucy's glare became a glower.

"I can handle her just fine," she retorted, obviously stung.

Rusty nodded soothingly. He hadn't meant to insult her. "Sure."

Just then his gelding decided to blast a whinny to its companion in a far pasture. The shrill noise surprised Baby, who jumped, then screwed up her eyes and began to wail. In seconds her face turned shrimp-red, and tears streamed down her plump cheeks.

"*Rusty*, how could you?" Lucy accused him in shocked tones.

She hugged the infant to her protectively—as if he'd let out the damned whinny himself!

"I didn't do anything," he said.

"You could have stopped him. Didn't you see he was going to do that?"

"Don't know how," he mumbled, at a loss. The child was crying in earnest now. "Sorry."

"And what *is* Baby's real name, anyway?" she asked above the wailing din.

He shrugged, suddenly feeling on the defensive. "We just call her Baby. I don't know if there's something formal on her birth certificate—or if she's even got one."

"She doesn't have a proper name?" Lucy demanded, shaming him. "I can't believe this." Stroking the child's head, Lucy rocked her back and forth. "Never mind. I'm going back to the house." Turning tail, she sent him one last disapproving glance that managed to make him feel lower than a slimy nightcrawler. He rubbed at the stubble on his cheeks, knowing she was right. Baby should have been given a real name long ago. He'd just always thought there was time. How had six months passed so quickly?

Lucy stalked away, her trim rear end twitching angrily in new blue jeans. Baby's cries calmed.

Rusty watched, perplexed at his reaction. Only moments before he'd been laughing at Lucy, feeling satisfyingly superior, but in two minutes she'd managed to cut him down to size. How had that happened?

Lucy fought down disappointment when Rusty carried his dinner plate into his office and shut the door with hushed finality. He stayed closeted in there all evening.

Then Fritzy announced she never ate before her favorite talk-show came on television at eleven-thirty. Since the efficient housekeeper had already bottle-fed the baby at six, then put her to bed for the night, Lucy was left alone.

Melancholy settled over her. This scattering at suppertime was not how she'd envisioned her "family" meals. Delicious though it was, she picked at her chicken and glanced around the empty room. In seconds she made up her mind to change things—at least a little—on the Lazy S.

A masculine face came at her. Fury flushed his skin ruddy, his features stiffened in an aggressive mask of anger. The familiar face, twisted in rage, snarled and shouted, called her *"Bitch."*

"No!" Lucy cried, cringing, "don't say that. I'm sorry. Please—"

The man ignored her pleas. Actually, he seemed to relish them, and his taunts became even more insulting. "You're stupid, you hear? You'd be nothing without me to straighten you out. Nothing! If people knew how incompetent you are at even the simplest tasks—why, they'd laugh."

Shoulders slumping, she felt the black void of anguish and despair threaten to engulf her. "I'll try harder next time," she defended weakly, already knowing it would do no good at all. "I won't burn your toast next time. I'll stand right by the toaster and watch the bread every second. It won't happen again."

He sneered at her. "You can't even do that right. You're useless!"

"Please stop," she heard herself whimper, the cry turning into a loud moan. "Please."

"Lucy," another voice called urgently. "Lucy, wake up."

Abruptly she awoke to total disorientation. Inside her chest her heart pounded furiously. The oily dampness of nervous perspiration filmed her body so that her nightgown stuck to her skin. Her eyes flew wide and she bolted up, gasped in lungfuls of air. For interminable seconds she didn't know where she was. The darkened room was alien, the bed different.

"Lucy," the new voice said calmly, "you were having a nightmare. It's okay. Wake up, now." Strong arms embraced her. Strangely, they didn't feel threatening. They were gentle, paternal. Tender.

The angry face faded. Slowly she recognized the voice. Rusty was sitting on the edge of her bed, stroking her back, patting her reassuringly. He was bare-chested, his warm pelt of dark hair soft against her cheek. Flannel pajama bottoms covered the rest of him. It was dark in the room.

Lucy stiffened. Rusty?

Coming fully awake, she glanced around. Neon digital numbers on the bedside clock read 12:03. Midnight. It always happened at midnight. For some reason that was the hour when Kenneth really got going. She shuddered.

"It's all right," Rusty crooned, beginning to rock her against his chest. His arms were welcoming, protective. She clutched his warm skin, taut with muscle. "The bogeyman's gone."

Bogeyman. A child's name for a frightening night-time specter. Only she was an adult, and her personal bogeyman had been so very real.

A pain that came from within clamped around her throat. She realized she was shaking, every part of her body trembling as if with a sick fever.

She wept then, tucked her face into the juncture of Rusty's neck where his stubble gave way to the softer skin of his collarbone. Choking back sobs, she clung to the man who offered comfort. When would she ever get over it? she wondered in despair. When would the bogeyman ever *really* go away?

Chapter Three

"It was Kenneth," Rusty said in a low voice. "Kenneth did this to you."

Still upset, Lucy shook her head, her hair falling into her eyes. "I don't want to talk about—"

"He hit you, didn't he?" Rusty demanded. Though his voice was quiet, she could hear outrage rumbling beneath his words like insurrectionists about to revolt.

"He—he didn't hit me. The things he said...they hurt worse than that."

He tilted his head, confused. "Your husband said mean things to you? That gave you a bad dream?"

In an effort to stop crying, she drew ragged breaths. "I know it's hard to understand. It's hard to explain." How she disliked sounding like a too-sensitive baby, spoiled and self-centered. She hadn't spoken about it with anyone except the therapist, and that had been difficult enough. She wasn't about to throw open the door to her soul's deepest secret. Not to Rusty; he wouldn't understand. No one would. No one could comprehend her reasons for staying with Kenneth during those bleak years of their marriage.

"Lucy—"

"Rusty, no, please. I...I can't." Moonlight, streaming in her window, carved shadows over the masculine lines of Rusty's face. In the darkness his brown eyes appeared black, penetrating.

His shoulders were big, his chest full, his abdomen ribbed. No man had held her for so long. She hadn't allowed it—or even wanted it—and certainly no half-dressed man. Lucy shut her eyes, overwhelmed.

With his big hands he stroked her arms from her shoulders to her wrists. As his palms glided over her skin, bared by her sleeveless gown, she could feel his work-hardened calluses, formed by honest labor. He was caressing her, she realized with a new shock. Rusty...caressing her?

He studied her, and she could almost feel him mentally probing for answers, answers she knew she couldn't give, didn't know if she *had* them to give. With her back to the window she hoped he couldn't see her well.

"You're not gonna talk about this with me, are you? Well, what happened to him, anyway? How did he die?" Before she could reply, his grip on her arms tightened, his voice roughened. "I wouldn't blame you if you had something to do with it."

Lucy gasped. "My God, no. It was his heart. He...he had a congenital defect. Both his brother and father did, too."

Rusty shrugged, brutally uncaring. "At least the creep left you well-off."

She bowed her head. "I guess I should thank you for coming in. Did...did I make a noise?"

"If you call an agonizing moan that could wake the next ranch ten miles over a 'noise,' then, yeah, you did."

"I apologize for waking you. I didn't mean to."

"Didn't you?" He grimaced at his own sarcasm. "You didn't mean to have a horrible nightmare and wake up sweating, shaking and sobbing? I'd have never guessed."

She could think of nothing to say.

He stood, and she wondered if it was only in her imagination that he did so reluctantly. "I'll go now. You'll be all right."

She nodded.

"But we're not finished with this. I won't push now, but soon…" He left the rest unsaid, stared at her meaningfully, strode out the door and shut it with a quiet click.

Hugging herself, Lucy felt an errant thought begin to bloom, unfurling like the petals of a flower. While she found Rusty gruff and uncompromising, he had rushed to her when she'd cried out, when she'd needed him.

Rusty had come to comfort her.

As if the night before had never happened, as if Lucy had never cried out in fear and Rusty had never consoled her with his voice and his touch, the next morning he barely spared her a glance when he entered the kitchen.

After pouring himself a mug of steaming coffee, he downed it in four gulps and turned to leave. Ribbons of sunlight fought with morning gloom to lance through the nook's high windows and fall on Rusty's hair. Streaks of russet Lucy hadn't seen before appeared in the thick waves.

At the stove Fritzy mixed thick batter.

"Good morning," Lucy said, trying to catch his eye. Before her sat orange juice and toasted waffles sprinkled with powdered sugar.

Grunting something unintelligible, he collected his hat from a wall hook.

"Um, what are you going to do today?"

"Work." He moved toward the door.

She wished she knew how to stop him. "Well, what should I do?"

His boots making staccato thuds on the hardwood floor, he was already out of the kitchen when his voice came back over his shoulder. "Whatever you want."

Lucy blinked, gazing sightlessly at the waffles. Well, what did she expect? The fact that he had come to her last night obviously meant little. Just as he would unemotionally soothe a frightened horse until it was composed, he'd soothed her until she was calm—all part of his duties.

"Another waffle, Lucy?" Fritzy asked.

"Thank you, Fritzy, but no. I'm really full." She didn't think she could get another bite past her suddenly constricted throat.

With Fritzy washing the breakfast dishes, Lucy agreed to carry the baby outside for air, "Just for a few minutes," Lucy clarified sternly. "Then you'll take the baby."

"Oh, of course, dear," Fritzy assured her, tightening her apron.

So, the blanket-wrapped child in her arms, Lucy stepped into the morning's crisp sunshine and glanced at the overgrown lawn. If Fritzy wouldn't allow her to help inside the house, she would begin outside.

A profound need to sculpt a place for herself, to be a valuable entity on the ranch burned inside her; she would do all in her power to make her dream come true.

Lucy wanted to be needed. She wanted to have a place where others counted on her. She wanted family...even if that family was comprised of only Fritzy, Baby...and Rusty.

Badly in need of a good mowing, the lawn would be a fine place to start making herself useful. With the men so busy branding, she guessed no one had time for this chore. Rusty's truck was gone, but down at the corrals she could see ropes whirling and the wispy trail of the branding fire. Faint bawling came to her over the breeze.

Fallen leaves made a colorful but messy canopy over the overgrown grass, and those would have to be raked first. Placing the child on the quilt safely out of harm's way, she spied a dented aluminum gardening shed shoved against the house's side wall and hunted through for tools. Sunlight warmed her back and sparkled on the last drops of dewy grass. Lucy hummed a country tune.

Hands on hips, she surveyed the tools she'd brought out—cotton canvas gloves, a rake and two plastic trash barrels. The mower she left in the shed for now. Good. As a young girl she'd performed yard work for spending money; she could do this. And she'd do it well. A person had to start somewhere, and although *starting* had never been her problem, this time she'd complete the job.

She'd make herself indispensable here. Essential. An

intrinsic cog in the Lazy S wheel. Hope filling her heart, she bent to collect the rake, when from the corner of her eye, she noticed the baby about to thrust something into her mouth.

Somehow she'd wriggled to the edge of the quilt and tugged out a tuft of grass. Lucy flew to her, put a halt to the grass lunch and lifted the child into her arms.

"Silly girl," Lucy scolded gently, cradling her, "grass is for cows, not humans. Now, you just lie quietly while I rake, all right?"

Settling the little imp down again on her stomach, she began to turn when the baby giggled, pulled her knees to her chest, and gave a rocking sort of scoot forward. Her face mashed into the blanketed ground but she only pushed herself up, grinning. Again, she pulled her knees under, swayed back and forth, and gave another hopping scoot.

"No, no, Baby." Lucy put her back in the middle of the quilt. Enjoying the new game, the child merely resumed her forward lurch. She looked like a grasshopper. Lucy watched, amazed and alarmed. Three more rocking hops and once again tiny fingers reached for the fascinating green spears. How was she to get any work done if every moment she had to tend this suddenly mobile tot?

Fritzy would have to help.

The growl of an engine kicking over sounded behind her, and Lucy whirled to see the elderly housekeeper behind the wheel of a ranch vehicle, a mud-spattered Range Rover.

"Wait!" Scooping up the baby, Lucy walked quickly toward the car. It was some fifty yards away. She called, "Where are you going?"

Fritzy waved, the car already rolling forward. "Got to do the grocery shopping. Be back in a few hours."

Lucy lurched into an awkward run, the child flopping uncomfortably in her arms. "But, you can't leave me *alone!*" Aghast, she nearly panicked. She had no idea what to do with a child for hours.

Fritzy swung the vehicle around the drive and stuck her head out the window. "Just put her down for a nap around noon, dear, right after you give her a bottle. I left it ready to warm in the kitchen." Her car picked up speed.

"But...but, I wanted to mow!"

"Use the playpen," came Fritzy's far-off reply. The retreating car trailed a plume of dust, disappeared in the thickly rising motes as if in a magical puff of smoke.

Coming to a halting stop, Lucy panted and shifted the thousand-pound infant onto her other hip. She thrust her hair from her eyes and blinked.

The baby stared expectantly into her face.

Lucy stared back. "Excuse me," she asked the child politely, "but where exactly is this playpen?"

"Hear you got a little gal livin' up with you, Rus," Beatrice said slyly, popping her gum. Her brassy blond hair was piled on top of her head a good six inches high, and the crimson lipstick painted over her lips framed two slightly buck teeth.

Rusty scowled up at her, ill-tempered from his restless night. It wasn't often he was jolted awake by the shocking reverberations of a woman's cry.

Because Beatrice was waiting, he said, "That 'little gal' just bought half the Lazy S, and she's my business partner, nothing more. Now that we've gotten past that, why don't you hustle your sassy behind over to get me some coffee?'' He darted a glance around the diner, urgently hoping the mining representative he was to meet would show up soon. He'd often done business at the roadside stop, which was a scant thirty miles from the ranch, and today he wanted to sew up the gypsum deal promptly so he could move on to other cash-raising ventures.

Beatrice grinned, chewed her gum and completely ignored his demand. ''Hear she's a looker, too, Rus. Black hair, green eyes. And where'd she get all that money? Folks're talking, you know.'' She waggled her penciled eyebrows at him, gesturing with her empty coffeepot at the diner's early-morning customers who were just straggling in.

''It's too early for this,'' Rusty growled, hunched over the cracked Formica counter. Irritable and on edge, he began to tear strips from a paper napkin. ''Just get the damn coffee.'' Two cowhands he knew who worked for a nearby feedlot clumped in, doffed their hats and took a booth. They raised a hand and he nodded.

''Sure, honey, soon's you tell me what's going on up there.'' Completely unintimidated by Rusty's glower, which normally cowed the toughest of hombres, Beatrice slid onto the next stool. Because everyone was accustomed to waiting until she was good and ready to serve them, the two cowhands sat patiently. ''Come on, Rusty, we grew up together, you and me. We even had a thing going when we were fifteen, remember?''

He almost smiled, remembering, but he didn't want to encourage her. The snoopiest waitress who ever gossiped across the face of Nevada, Beatrice loved intrigue. Indeed, people came from miles around for her always hot, but mud-thick coffee and her sympathetic ear. Her advice was also invariably sound. What set her further apart, Rusty grudgingly admitted, was that when she had to, Beatrice could keep a secret.

He liked her, actually; considered her a good friend. There'd been a time or two he'd confided in her himself. He just didn't want to discuss his new partner.

She leaned close. "So, what's her name?"

He gave an elaborate shrug. The napkin was in six pieces now. "Lucy."

"Lucy, huh? And this Lucy's already gotten under your skin. She must be something."

Rusty reared back, about to correct her, when he caught himself. Beatrice loved to lay well-meaning traps. "I'll have eggs, scrambled, some of those pan-fried potatoes and three rashers of bacon."

The woman pursed her lips. "I'm glad you've got somebody finally. Since those brothers of yours passed away it's been hard on you, I know. A man needs a pretty woman waitin' for him at home—somebody to warm his bed." Her grin turned wicked.

"Coffee, Bea," Rusty warned. If he hadn't already had those kinds of thoughts about Lucy, Beatrice's needling probably wouldn't bother him. Where was the damned mining rep, anyway? Restless, he glanced at the door again.

The bell on the glass front sounded its tinny ring as two more customers entered. Neither was his man. He sighed.

Reluctantly Bea got to her feet. "Listen, you bring Lucy on out here, all right? She sounds real nice."

Making no reply, Rusty was glad to get her off his

back. He put up a hand to the two new men and resumed shredding the napkin.

It was only later, when the napkin resembled confetti, that he realized—he never did get any coffee.

Rusty pulled his battered pickup into the gravel drive and cut the engine with a satisfied grunt of accomplishment. The gypsum deal finalized, he could look forward to at least a modest stream of cash. He hadn't considered the notion before, because the profits wouldn't have come soon enough to pay the mortgage, and the amounts weren't that impressive. But things were different now. Every penny would count.

At only noon on the first day of his deal with Lucy Donovan, he'd already taken the first step toward his objective, and their contract wasn't even drawn up yet. There would be no changing of grant deeds or titles for now—he and Lucy had agreed that would happen at the end of the year—but only *if* he failed to come up with the required amount.

That *if* would never be.

Slamming the truck's door behind him, he started for the corrals. From a hundred yards away, he could see the men had made good progress, with almost all the late calves marked and the older cows culled. For the space of several heartbeats, he hesitated, allowed himself a brief, treasured moment.

To some, the arid desert beyond the ranch outbuildings might appear barren and lifeless. Rusty knew better. To him, the land whispered its beauty, rather than shouted it. It took a discerning eye to appreciate the embracing framework of the Humboldt range, the flash of the bluebird's breast as it winged past, the spicy scent of sagebrush and creosote. In not too many months hence, Rusty knew, wild violets would sway in the spring breezes that would comb the region, and then he'd be able to plant alfalfa and barley fields, revel in watching them grow green and tall.

Rusty knew he was a man of the land. In the West it was tradition for a large ranch like the Lazy S to pass first to the eldest son. Should he die, the next son in line inherited. In the prior century, often there would be enough work to support everyone, but in modern times of low beef prices and high production costs, there wasn't enough income for all three of the Sheffield boys.

Rusty always understood this, accepted it without rancor, and of necessity he sought a different career for himself. He'd been the only son to attend college, earn a degree and move to the city.

With two older brothers, he'd never expected, as Lucy had succinctly pointed out, to have the place to himself. In the blink of an eye, he mused, a life could irrevocably change.

Although he'd striven to carve out a San Francisco law career for himself and he'd succeeded, hadn't he always known, somewhere deep inside, that he belonged *here*, working with animals and soil—in this place which spoke to him? No, he didn't miss the law. Not when he could be what he'd always dreamed about—a rancher.

At the corrals, Harris, the fortyish, quietly competent foreman he'd left in charge, dismounted and led his horse to the rail.

"Boss." Harris gave Rusty a laconic nod. His enormous handlebar mustache that drooped over the corners of his mouth lent him a perpetually mournful appearance. "The calves are big this year. Should get a good sale out of 'em."

Rusty hooked a boot on the bottom rung. "That early-summer rain kept the forage green a long time," he acknowledged, "kept the mamas making good milk. I don't know about the sale, though. Beef prices are still down."

Inside the corral, a newly roped calf, startled and confused, turned back toward the mounted cowboy who'd roped it and tried to run beneath the horse's belly. The annoyed horse crow-hopped sideways; in seconds his movements escalated into wild, full-fledged bucking. The surprised young cowboy barely hung on.

Seeing this, the other men instantly started hooting, catcalling to the rider in the good-natured ribbing common to ranch hands.

"You couldn't ride a rail fence in a stiff breeze, boy," shouted the man holding a still-smoking branding iron.

"Stick him," yelled another encouragingly. "Stick him like a postage stamp."

Harris grinned at Rusty. "That horse'll soon have Ranny grassed," and within seconds the cowhand called Ranny sailed off his mount in an unscheduled flight.

Ranny pulled himself slowly to his feet, spitting out dirt and clutching handfuls of something he didn't want. Red-faced, yet clearly unhurt, he dusted himself off and stomped after his horse.

Seeing his embarrassment, the others razzed him unmercifully, and to Ranny's credit, he merely collected the trailing reins of his mount, soothed the animal and then stopped in the center of the corral. Sheepish, he raised his head. "You know, I flew so high, it was damn scary without wings."

Men clapped him on the back and chuckled.

But Rusty frowned. In all the teasing, something seemed empty, missing. It was as it ought to be—the branding—the man bantering, so familiar, and yet...

The truth slammed into him. Tom and Landon should be there.

Rusty swallowed thickly, the memories of other brandings washing over him in a painful tide. His oldest brother Tom had been the finest roper in the family, winning buckles and modest jackpots at area competitions, while next-in-line Landon had loved to ride the roughstock. When they were teenagers, feisty Landon had broken several bones getting bucked off wild bulls and ornery broncs. Rusty had idolized them both.

When they had all grown to manhood and their father passed on, Tom and Landon had always invited Rusty back for roundups, expected him to come, and of course he had.

"Sure do miss the boys," Harris commented, echoing Rusty's thoughts. He gave his mustache an awkward tug. "Don't seem right somehow, without 'em."

Rusty cleared his throat, tight with memories. "Yeah." Abruptly he pivoted and headed for the house. The men could finish. It was time he quit mooning about things he couldn't change and get on with what he could.

Anyway, what did it matter, Rusty thought bleakly? In the space of a heartbeat, his brothers were gone, and he was unexpectedly left with the ranch...and now with Lucy Donovan's unwanted involvement.

He forced himself to shove his grief into a shadowed corner where the harsh glare of attention wouldn't illuminate it so painfully. Because his head was lowered, he didn't see the tableau before him until he came upon it.

Two filled-to-bursting trash barrels, tilted drunkenly against the cottonwood tree, dripped papery leaves, twigs and fresh-mowed grass. A rake, an edger and the mower lay scattered about, along with two apparently flung-off gloves. The lawn itself was immaculate.

The baby's playpen had been set a safe distance away, but she wasn't inside. When he got closer, he peered around the trunk of the shading cottonwood.

Lucy knelt on a spread-out patchwork quilt, making silly noises. Dirt streaked across her cheek and clippings clung to her hair. She didn't see him. Still twenty yards off, Rusty stopped.

"That's a girl," Lucy encouraged in ridiculously syrupy tones, reserved only for very young children, "come on, come on, you little cricket."

Grinning hugely and drooling with pleasure, the baby shrieked and made a sort of scampering bound forward. Rusty raised his eyebrows. He didn't know she'd learned to move around yet.

"Good baby!" Lucy cried, clapping her hands. "Good Cricket. Come to Lucy. Here we go. Come on." She patted her knees, folded under her, and when the child took another scoot forward, Lucy sang out praise, grabbing her up to swing overhead. The infant squealed in delight.

Something inside Rusty loosened, like a heavy rock breaking away from a great cliff. He was aware of drawing breath in slow, fulfilling draughts. Time slowed. His shoulders began to relax, his tension fading away with his grieving memories.

He couldn't take his eyes off Lucy.

There was something elemental, something that spoke to the primordial man in him that the scene was *right*. A woman, down on the grassy earth with a child, encouraging the baby to move, to progress. In a crazy flash of prescience he'd never owned, scenes strobed before his mind's eye—under this woman's care his beloved brother's child thrived, grew healthy. Strong.

He shook his head, and the images vanished, but the scene before him did not.

Silhouetted against the old ranch house, the sun glossing her hair to shiny coal, bringing rosiness to her cheeks, Lucy, Rusty realized, was magnificent. Last night in her bedroom he'd been surprised at the rush of protectiveness he felt toward her. Her nightgown's thin white fabric did not preserve her modesty; he could see the uprisings of her nipples, and when he'd held her, could feel the soft contours of her breasts, could feel them pressing into his bare chest. Her breasts had felt like they were branding him...burning... burning.

Rusty didn't want to, but he couldn't help it; he ached with wanting her.

Wind trailed past, captured the scent of growing things and sunshine.

Lucy felt her arms begin to twinge with the effort of swinging the baby overhead, and lowered her down. As she turned, she spotted Rusty, who had the look of someone who'd been there awhile. Her heart gladdened. Had he been there long? Did he see the baby's new trick?

Turning fully, she hugged the infant to her chest and was about to ask him, when she was caught by his expression.

Beneath the brim of his dark hat, Rusty's normally

stern features seemed open and unguarded. He was looking at her with an approving, admiring stare that settled around Lucy like a deliciously cozy blanket on a frigid day.

She stilled.

She'd been cold for so terribly long, she thought in a kind of sad wonder, her life a wasteland of isolation and loneliness. But Rusty Sheffield had the power to warm her all the way down to her soul.

Rusty had the power, she realized suddenly, to break her heart.

Chapter Four

Lucy's hand trembled on the baby's back. She was still kneeling on the patchwork quilt. As she gazed into Rusty's warm expression, a little explosion of delight bloomed within her. Try as she might, she could not quell it.

"Uh, hello there," she said, suddenly struck shy. "Did you see the baby's new trick?"

He came forward, and when he reached the edge of the quilt, he knelt down opposite her and rested his hands on his powerful thighs. She tried not to stare at the bunched muscles that strained against the worn denim fabric of his jeans. Her breath grew short.

"You mean *Cricket's* new trick?" he teased.

She flushed. "I just called her a cricket because her little hops remind me of a grasshopper. I might have said bunny rabbit, or kangaroo or anything else that jumps around."

"I like the name," he said, ignoring her comment.

"Cricket." He sounded the word aloud again, as if considering it. "It suits her."

"But it's not a name," Lucy protested.

"Why not? Put her down," he instructed. "See if she can make it to me."

With exasperated amusement Lucy complied, laying the infant on her stomach. "You just can't call her that."

"Why not?" he said again.

Seeing Rusty, the child chortled and immediately started to lurch toward him. "Come on, Cricket," he coaxed in gentle tones. "Come to your old uncle Rus."

"It's an insect, you know," Lucy reminded him. "A...a bug."

"Tom would have liked it," Rusty countered quietly. He took off his hat, lifted the baby to his broad chest and nuzzled her plump neck.

Something about the natural way he handled the child touched her. *Rusty would make a fantastic father,* she thought. Patient and kind and very loving. In fact, he was already doing wonderfully with Cricket. She studied him and wondered at her sudden vulnerability. She felt weak and was trembling, as if she'd just engaged in strenuous activity. Her insides melted, like sun-warmed honey. Blood heated and pooled in her abdomen and lower; it pulsed in unmentionable places.

A gust of wind ruffled Rusty's hair, and she found herself wishing she could touch the silky brown locks. Rich amber highlights glinted in the strands. At his open shirt collar, his throat revealed a few darker hairs.

With a rush of memory she recalled his bare chest pressed to her when she was wearing only a thin nightgown. Beneath her cotton blouse her breasts grew weighty, and the low pounding in her veins beat in her ears, sounding an ancient rhythm deep inside her body's core. Her breath soughed shallowly in her chest, and a strange, excited sort of lethargy gripped her.

She wanted him.

Rusty glanced up, stared into her eyes. His own sharpened, the brown color enriching to smoky toffee. Slowly his gaze lowered to her parted lips. She saw him take in her shallow breathing and then lower his gaze still further to her breasts. Forbidden thrills sparked through her like sheet lightning. He wanted to touch her, she could tell. He wanted to touch her breasts. She gasped softly.

His attention rose back to her eyes while a communication—urgent, personal, profound—hummed between them.

"*Lucy,*" he whispered, his voice husky with promise.

Gooseflesh rose up, lifting the hair on her arms. Her nipples beaded stiffly. She had to fight off the shiver that threatened to flash down her spine—a shiver that had nothing to do with the air temperature, and everything to do with the pure, predatory interest stamped on his features.

Predatory? A stray breeze whistled past, and this time Lucy did shiver. Without thinking, she crossed her arms protectively.

No, not him. She'd already experienced *that* aspect of a male-female relationship, and she remembered the self-doubt and insecurity that accompanied it. Her mind shied away from the intimate memories of her marriage. *You couldn't please a man if you tried,* the angry voice echoed through time. *You've never satisfied me.*

Deliberately she glanced away from Rusty, breaking the bond of awareness that stretched taut.

As if he had read her mind, he cleared his throat and handed the baby back. "Got work to do," he muttered, and rose to his feet. He scowled, abruptly becoming the brusque man she recognized. His distance was an unbreachable barrier, a barricade she could never surmount. Was she so transparent? Could he somehow have divined her private thoughts?

At the unnerving possibility, something inside her shriveled. She clutched the baby.

Resetting his hat, he stared at the middle distance. "One of our neighbours wants to lease a percentage of our water, so I'm gonna meet with him pretty soon. He owns a paint store, so we'll swap part of the payment for enamel, and the barns can get a fresh coat."

Lucy digested this. She knew he was interested in bringing quick capital to the bank account—to buy her out at year's end, not that he really could.

But she focused on one word. She stood, anchored the child on her left hip and ignored her overheated body. "Did you say paint? Will there be any extra gallons left?"

"What do you want paint for?" His eyes narrowed.

Shrugging, she shifted the baby to her front, just to keep her hands busy. She didn't want Rusty thinking she was demanding. Any hint of such would have sent Kenneth into a rage. How often had he said she was ungrateful...and too needy? How many times had he accused her of always wanting more, more, more! *"Don't I give you enough? Don't I love you more than anyone in the world?"* His bitter voice reverberated in her head, brought on violent, soul-killing memories. For a panicked moment she was afraid she might cry.

Rusty waited. "I asked what you wanted with paint?"

He wouldn't understand anything of what went on in her mind, and in fairness, she didn't expect him to. *Just ask him, Lucy,* she scolded herself.

Hating her meek tone, she swallowed hard and half whispered, "I...I just wondered...if the house could have a coat, too."

"Oh." He hunched a shoulder away and inspected the structure with a grim expression. "The house needs it, I guess. There'll probably be enough." With that he strode toward the front door, probably to seal himself in his office and make endless business calls. She watched his purposeful strides take him away, and she felt bereft.

She dragged in a long, difficult breath. Her counselor had encouraged her to assert herself. Months of therapy had helped, but not enough, Lucy now realized. Not nearly enough. She bent to collect the quilt. Then Lucy managed to drag the overfilled trash barrels to the back of the house and replace the gardening tools—a difficult task while still holding Cricket.

She was a bit more confident than she'd been six months ago, although she knew there was still a long way to go. At least she'd gotten Rusty to agree to let her paint. And she'd learned that she could feel desire for a man. For Rusty.

It wasn't good.

She should have known that her memories of his kindness as a youth and her longing for a real home would be all bound up together. She should have recognized that they would inextricably tangle to entrap her in fierce yearning.

"This is absurd," she muttered, annoyed with her thoughts. This was stupid. As time passed, wouldn't these feelings fade naturally? Wasn't what she was experiencing merely a leftover crush from childhood? Of course it would all go away if only she concentrated on other things. She wanted to improve her horsemanship skills, for instance. And she wanted to make a trip into Reno, buy a few items for Cricket's room.

Inside the coolness of the house, she heated formula for the baby's noon bottle as Fritzy had instructed her, hoping she'd gotten it right, and sat on the davenport. Cricket greedily stretched out her hands for the plastic bottle and yelled, *"Yamaschoo,"* the infant translation for milk, Lucy reasoned.

Laying her downy head across Lucy's bent arm, Cricket grasped the bottle and did all the work, and Lucy felt an unfamiliar peacefulness settle around her. Everything would be fine, she thought. Probably in only a short while they would all become accustomed to one another.

But she wouldn't stop there, she decided, forcing herself to look ahead. She had another goal.

"Cricket needs the family together at mealtimes," Lucy stated to both Fritzy and Rusty early that evening. She'd deliberately ambushed them when she saw Rusty go into the kitchen for a soda while Fritzy finished cooking dinner. She barred the doorway with her body. "At least for the evening meal. She deserves as normal a childhood as possible." Raising her chin with false bravado, she lifted Cricket from the floor where she was gnawing on a pile of rubber blocks and hoped no one noticed her anxiety. Rarely did Lucy put herself forward, and acquiring this new skill took a considerable measure of courage.

"But I need to eat late, dear," Fritzy said, pausing in the act of stirring an enormous pot of split-pea and ham soup. The fragrant scent of garlic toast wafted throughout the kitchen.

"And I need to work," Rusty added. "In my office."

"No." Although her voice quavered at facing them down, she refused to back off. "Shared family meals are what normal, healthy people do," she said defiantly. "Cricket needs the stability of everyday routines." The fact that Lucy, herself, needed and wanted at least the illusion of family was something she would keep to herself.

She wasn't above using Fritzy's and Rusty's affection for the child to achieve her own goal. "No," she repeated, "you both *want* to eat alone, or at other times, but you don't need to. Cricket, however, *needs* us all together. She's a growing child," she added as another inducement.

"When my Henry was alive, we always ate at a late hour," Fritzy stated emphatically, ladling Lucy's soup into a stoneware tureen.

A dim memory came back to Lucy. "Don't you have a son, Fritzy?"

The housekeeper glanced at her, wary now. "Yes. Paul lives in Canada with his family now, though."

"That's nice." Lucy smiled reassuringly. "And when he was growing up—did you and your Henry take meals with him?"

"Well, of course," Fritzy sputtered. "But that was years ago—"

"And Paul is a fine father to his children," she guessed. "He and his wife do try to eat with them?" She let the question make her point for her.

Fritzy's brow took on a troubled frown. "I suppose."

"You're like a mother to Cricket, you know."

"Goodness, not a mother," Fritzy exclaimed, flustered but pleased at the comment. She amended, "Like a grandmother, maybe."

"A grandmother, then." Lucy had no problem with that. "An important part of her family."

Fritzy made a weak sound of agreement.

Rusty grimaced, but she could see she was getting to him, too. "You're the only father she knows," Lucy told him. "If Tom were alive, he'd eat dinner with her, you can bet on that." She faced him square on, hoping the invocation of Tom's name would help. Cricket made a grab for her nose. Without thinking, she avoided the grasping fingers.

Rusty let out a long breath; it sounded like a sigh.

Yes! she shouted inwardly. *I've won this round!*

Accepting the bowl of steaming soup, Lucy beamed at Fritzy. "Well, then, shall we all have a seat?" Before they could protest, she marched to the table, then rummaged for three soup spoons, napkins and milk glasses. "Fritzy, you go right ahead ladling out the soup. I'll get Cricket's bottle and baby cereal. Rusty, can you fetch the bread?"

He grumbled something unintelligible, and Fritzy made a harrumphing noise.

Lucy pretended not to notice their shared glance of defeat. When they all were seated, with Cricket safely buckled into a high chair and noisily slamming her arms onto the plastic tray, Lucy smiled at everyone and began to ask innocent, pleasant questions about their day.

As they replied, reluctantly at first, and then with increasing ease, she felt a welling up of triumph and pleasure in her chest. Rusty soon relaxed and shared

with them details about his plans to upgrade the herd.
The soup tasted better to her than any food had in
months. Her heart lightened, and she even made a few
awkward attempts to help Fritzy get cereal into
Cricket's mouth. The gooey stuff got on Lucy's hand,
made streaks on her blouse, and a blob even ended up
in her hair. She was surprised to find she actually didn't
mind.

She had the beginnings of a family.

Rusty pushed himself to exhaustion from long before
dawn to long after dark. He'd made the small concession to Lucy to take the evening meal together as a
"family" as she liked to call them. It wasn't so bad,
he admitted grudgingly, and in the long run Cricket
would probably benefit.

But the idea made him uncomfortable, and he didn't
know exactly why except that Lucy wasn't family. She
was merely the woman who'd bought half his ranch,
and only for one year's time because that was all he
was going to allow. And they were not related in any
way. That their parents had been briefly married in the
distant past did not bind them at all.

His physical responses to her could be controlled. At
thirty, he was no randy youth ruled by his libido, but
a man, grown—with a man's judgment and restraint.
The desire he felt for Lucy was inappropriate, unwanted and unwise, but it would definitely pass.

The problem was a minor one, easily dismissed, and
each time he thought about it, he simply pushed himself harder at whatever task was at hand, be it digging
post holes or dickering with a mining company for
mineral rights to his land, or grinding through endless
paperwork. Sometimes he was even successful.

Lucy had been a resident in his home for nearly a month when he finally admitted that she was an incredibly hard worker. In his hurried comings and goings he saw her scrubbing the baseboards over Fritzy's protests, and she'd actually regrouted the loose tiles in his bathroom with a tube of silicone she'd found on his workbench.

Without his noticing, Lucy had assumed more and more child-care duties. And the sight of her with the baby firmly attached to her hip had become familiar around the ranch.

At the end of her fourth week at the Lazy S, he'd just dismounted from a ride to check the valuable ranch bulls, when he came upon her cleaning and bandaging a barbwire injury for Harris.

Cricket was probably napping in the house, and most of the men were occupied repairing tractor engines, digging out clogged water holes or stringing new wire fences—the grinding but necessary winter ranch work. The afternoon's bright sunlight held a cold fall sharpness, reminding him that winter waited impatiently to close her fist on the land.

Lucy's shiny hair fell across her cheek as she leaned over the jagged scratch that rent the foreman's arm. His sleeve was rolled high so she could work, revealing tough, knotted biceps. It appeared to Rusty that Harris was flexing the muscle unnecessarily.

"And you need a tetanus shot," Lucy scolded the man, snipping a length of white adhesive tape to hold the gauze she'd wrapped around his arm. Her small hands on the brawny foreman's biceps looked delicate and very feminine. "We can't have you getting sick."

Harris grinned, showing all his teeth, quite a feat considering the impressive size of his drooping mustache. He leaned his good arm on the corral rail behind him in supreme nonchalance.

"Yes, ma'am," he agreed so readily that Rusty scowled in amazement. "And thank you kindly. Sure is nice of you to patch me up." Normally Harris kept to himself, didn't go to Reno chasing after women like some of the cowboys. Still, Rusty could see Harris enjoyed the fussing, and he was annoyed beyond all reason when the other man lingered.

"Go on," Rusty ordered the man sharply. "Go see Doc Miller right now and get the damned shot."

Glancing from Lucy to Rusty, Harris gave a reluctant nod.

Meeting Lucy's startled gaze, Rusty gave her only a hard look, then stomped away, pulling his gelding.

At the barn's big doors, he threw the latch back with a bang. There was no denying that his men liked her, enjoyed her company. It was remarkable how she'd integrated herself into all their lives so quickly.

An inordinate number of minor wounds among the men required her immediate medical attention, Rusty noticed. It was unbelievable how often they were getting hurt. Fritzy had even had to purchase an additional first aid kit, what with the rapid depletion of the supplies. He snorted. They were all sniffing around Lucy like a pack of coyotes in mating season, snarling among themselves for her attention—at the same time acting like wimps at the slightest scratch. They were making damn fools of themselves.

Not that he could blame them, if he were honest. Whenever Lucy appeared, she brought with her a happy charisma, despite whatever turns her past had taken. Her happiness was magically contagious, infecting those around with a new lightness of heart, with smiles and laughter.

From the shadowed barn doorway, he watched her pack up scissors, tape and antibiotic ointment. With the toe of his boot he kicked at a dirt clod and wondered about her past. She never spoke of it, and whenever anyone mentioned anything about the subject it somehow got changed. Kenneth Donovan must have been a real prize. Rusty was suddenly and fiercely glad he was dead. Lucy had evidently been treated shabbily, and she didn't deserve that. Petite, fragile, skittish Lucy deserved a gentle hand, a man who'd take care of her.

From her post of the fence, she tossed him a shy smile, tucked the kit beneath her arm and headed back to the house. He didn't smile in return, merely dragged the heavy doors open and stripped the saddle from his gelding.

It was only because he could never resist an enigma that his thoughts centered on Lucy so frequently. She still shied like a spooked mare when he made a sudden movement, and at times her eyes flashed with a disturbing emotion he couldn't define. And then she'd lower her lashes, her features schooled into careful blankness. He had the impression she was hiding parts of herself, keeping secrets.

The mystery surrounding her tantalized him.

That evening, in the dead of night, he woke up, thinking he wanted water. Dim moonlight marbled over his dresser, the end of his bed, glinted off the brass doorknob. Wearing only his boxers, he put his feet on the cool, hardwood floor and let himself out of his room.

At Lucy's closed bedroom door he paused and forgot

all about the water. Through the wood, he could hear
gentle breathing. He imagined her wearing her thin
white nightgown, spread across the bed with uncon-
scious sensual grace. Her arms and legs would be bare,
the gown might even be hiked up to her thighs. Like
on the night she'd cried out and he'd comforted her,
he could see the dark areolas of her nipples, peaked
and calling to the man in him.

Rusty shut his eyes, leaned his forehead against the
doorjamb and felt his blood stirring. Erotic scenes of
Lucy beckoning him into her room, into her bed,
and…finally, into her body, consumed him. It would
be so easy to lift her nightgown, smooth his hands up
her lithe body, take her breast into his mouth. And in
his mind he was probing at her body's entrance, his
manhood hard as a pike staff, and rocking her, thrusting
until they both catapulted into a space filled with wonder and brilliant, bursting constellations.

Barefoot in the hallway shadows, he stood there
wanting Lucy: fully, achingly aroused and frustrated
and feeling like an idiot but completely unable to help
himself. The temptation to slip into her room was
nearly overwhelming; his hand actually lifted to turn
the knob when he gritted his teeth and lowered it back
to his side.

Outside, a male cicada chirped in search of a female.

For the first time, he questioned his ability to manage
things between them. Lucy's vulnerability, her need to
trust, her need for love shone so clearly from her ex-
pressive eyes. He was certain she wasn't aware of this,
but it was easy to recall the silent, lonely child she'd
been. Back then, his heart had gone out to her, though
he'd had little time to do anything about helping her,

and his fifteen-year-old mind wouldn't have known how, anyway.

But, damn it, she still affected him, made something come alive inside him.

It ate at him, her need, when he knew that he could not give her all a woman like her would want—or deserved. He felt obliged to guard her from the other men of the ranch, from the disappointments of the world…and now even from himself.

He *was* an idiot. He knew it, and the idea made helpless anger twist inside his chest. But he realized he could no more stop wanting Lucy than he could stop night from falling or dawn light from spearing up over the Humboldts. Without getting any water, and without holding Lucy in his arms, he forced himself back to his room and stretched out tensely on the bed.

Winging south along Interstate 80 in her sleek sports car, Lucy drove to Reno and was back by late afternoon, tired, but pleased with her purchases. Because she'd left the top down, her hair was wind tossed, her cheeks color stung. She felt great. Although she could have gone into nearby Lovelock, she wasn't confident the small town would have everything she wanted.

Loaded down with packages, she hurried into the house and couldn't wait to see Cricket and dress her in one of the darling new outfits she'd bought.

In moments Fritzy was oohing and ahhing over a three-foot stuffed bear, and the living room was strewn with shopping bags.

When Rusty strode into the house on his way to his office, he stopped dead at the open doorway and stared at the packages carelessly scattered over the davenport and around the floor.

"I've always adored sailor outfits," Fritzy was saying, holding up miniature white-and-blue-striped bib overalls, sewn with a red scarf.

"And did you see the denim jeans and Western boots? She'll be our little cowgirl!" Between packages on the davenport, Lucy sat happily bouncing Cricket on her lap.

"What the hell's all this?" Rusty bellowed, halfway into the room. Fists on his hips, he stood frowning at clothing, bears and a molded plastic toy box. Both Lucy and Fritzy jumped.

"I...I, um, picked up a few things for Cricket in Reno this morning," Lucy answered. Had she done something wrong?

"Why'd you do that?" he demanded.

"Her jammies were too small," Fritzy rushed to explain. "And all her other things were stretched to the limit. The baby had to have some clothes. She's growing, Rusty."

"I know." His tone was tinged with belligerence. "But I could have gotten whatever Cricket needs. We don't want anybody's charity." His expression was mutant, and with a sinking heart Lucy understood that "anybody" meant her. He felt threatened and made inadequate by her gesture. She hadn't considered Rusty at all when she'd chosen things; she'd only thought about Cricket's needs and of how she could fill them. Rusty's masculine ego was wounded. They both knew she had more money than he did—a great deal more. Her gesture had pointed that out.

Sensing the tense undercurrents in the room, Cricket howled and then started to cry. Although she didn't know what to do, Lucy automatically pressed the baby to her chest and whispered assurances until the child quieted.

Rusty was angry, just as Kenneth would have been. Lowering her gaze, she felt the familiar shrinking of her deepest self, the diminishing of her esteem.

"I was just…I thought it would be okay." Inside, her feelings warred, but she pushed on. "There wasn't much in her room, no real toys or mobiles or cuddly blankets." Hoping he wouldn't notice until she got herself under control, she bounced the baby on her lap and swallowed hard.

"Hell," he muttered.

Long heartbeats of silence drummed loud in her ears. Lucy could feel the weight of Rusty's gaze, but dared not lift her own. It took all her concentration to hold back the distressing tide of emotion. She felt rather than saw him studying the new things.

"That pink rig she had on yesterday was pretty tight," he said grudgingly. Reaching out, he fingered a soft cotton bedsack. "Her toes were all curled up in the foot part."

"Indeed, they were," Fritzy agreed, a gentle rebuke in her voice. She began folding outfits and tidying up. When she had a small stack, she headed for the stairs, to Cricket's room.

Lifting a white stuffed bunny with floppy ears, Rusty came around the sofa to stand before Lucy. In his brown calloused hand the feminine toy looked alien. He bent over and used it to tickle Cricket's ear. "I guess a baby ought to have playthings and clothes that fit."

"That's all I meant, Rusty," Lucy got out. A fine tremor shook her fingers. "I'm sorry if I—"

"No." He cut his hand through the air, straightening. Dragging off his hat, he turned it over and stared into the crown as if the words he wanted were written on the bottom. "I ought to be the sorry one, snapping at you like that. I've been working hard. I'm just tired and cross." He looked down at her, still seated on the sofa. "You did the right thing, Lucy. Thanks."

As if in a dream, Lucy lifted her head; she could barely credit what she was hearing. Rusty had verbally attacked her, questioned her motives. And then he'd listened to reason, decided he'd been wrong and simply apologized. There was no more shouting, he didn't rage for hours. He'd even praised her efforts. It was easy. Simple. Rational. The entire conversation astounded her.

He'd taken responsibility and apologized.

It was something Kenneth had never done.

Oh, he'd begged for forgiveness—and done so profusely. Right after he'd wounded her self-worth until she was nothing more than a quivering lump of flesh. When his rage was spent, all his harsh, biting words said…then, he'd weep.

Always afterward Kenneth was so abjectly sorry, so remorseful. Like a little boy, he would lay his head on her lap and plead for absolution. Never again would he hurt her. Never again would he treat her with anything but the utmost respect, the most tender care.

These were the times she could almost believe she loved him. This was the way she'd wished Kenneth would always be.

Because Lucy so desperately wanted Kenneth's promises to be true, because she was trapped by her lack of job skills and the confidence to make it on her own, because he'd drilled into her that she was worthless and no one else would want her, because she knew

no other options, she would minimize the abuse, ultimately accept responsibility for her husband's anger,
and she would forgive.

But sooner or later the cycle would always, always,
always begin again.

Maybe, just maybe, Rusty wasn't like that. In her
logical heart, she knew that all men didn't behave as
Kenneth had. But how was one to tell? The risk a
woman took in trusting a man was enormous. And she
had proven to herself that her own instincts were not
sound. She sighed and hugged Cricket, who had been
quietly playing with her fingers and whose eyelids were
beginning to droop.

If only there were some way to tell, some test or
barometer, some way to measure a man's character, his
integrity, his inner worth. But she knew of none, and
until one turned up, she could not afford to take that
risk again.

Each morning after breakfast Rusty hurried to his
work while Lucy took gloves, a scraper and a stack of
rough-gauge sandpaper and attacked the peeling eaves.
Each day she worked until noon. Sometimes she carted
the playpen outside and kept Cricket nearby for company. At other times, Fritzy watched the baby. Except
for the eaves and window frames, most of the home
was made of stucco, so she was able to complete the
sanding of all wood surfaces in just under a week.

She found the new paint that Rusty had bartered
from the neighbor, all stacked neatly in the garage. She
took two gallon cans, two brushes and a roller. Standing halfway up a wobbly aluminum ladder, she'd been
applying the eggshell enamel for nearly two hours
when Rusty came striding around the corner.

"Good God," he exclaimed, mouth dropping open as he took in the scene of Cricket, snoozing peacefully in her shaded playpen and a paint-spattered Lucy perched on the ladder. "What are you *doing?*"

"Oh, Rusty," she said, smiling down at him. She adjusted the paint cap she'd pulled on backward to keep her hair out of her eyes, and when her hand brushed her face, she felt wet paint streak across her nose. Darn it, she thought, that was the third time. She must look a mess.

"I figure I'll have the work done within five or six days. It'll look wonderful, don't you think?"

"You're painting the house? I thought you meant you wanted to have it done—not do the work yourself." He shook his head in amazement.

"Everybody else is too busy," she explained. "I'm not, so I figured I was the logical choice. You like it...don't you?"

"Lucy, you're working too hard," he stated sternly. "What makes you think you have to take on every job around here? My men will finish this." Coming forward, he put a hand on the ladder and his other on her calf. The ladder wobbled. "Why, this isn't even safe."

At his touch Lucy went still. She liked the feel of his strong hand on her body, even if it was only her leg, and even if her leg was covered by old jeans. Alarm, mixed with pleasure, spread through her in a frightening rush.

"You need a day off," Rusty was saying. "Away from work. I think maybe...a picnic." He rubbed his jaw. "Yeah, that sounds about right. Tomorrow we'll ride over to the river, take some food."

"A picnic?" she echoed, still frozen on the ladder. *Alone with Rusty, away from others.* From the corner of her eye, she darted a nervous glance at him. How well did she really know Rusty Sheffield? How smart would it be to put herself in a situation like that?

"Yeah, a picnic," he repeated. "You know—a little trip with food, lots of sunshine, relaxation?"

"I know what it is," she mumbled. Suddenly she was able to move, and she scrambled down the ladder, began to fit the lid on the paint can and collect supplies.

"Man, you're as nervous as a long-tailed cat under a rocking chair." Hands on hips, he watched her. "Why?"

"I'm not nervous," she lied. "I'm just busy. Very, very busy."

"But tomorrow you'll come, right?"

"Tomorrow I'll still be real busy. I've got Cricket to care for, you know. And your men are occupied with their jobs. I'll just finish the painting, if that's all right."

He considered her, his gaze raking her features, while she kept her face averted. "You're afraid," he accused. "You're terrified of going somewhere with me. What's the matter, do you think I'm going to jump you?"

"N-no. Of course not." He was too perceptive, too shrewd by half. She could not bring herself to look at him. "There's just so much I need to do."

"That's why it's important to get away. Call it time to recharge."

Lucy could tell Rusty was trying not to sound exasperated. She didn't reply, but kept her hands busy rolling up the drop cloth.

"Lucy, it's for me, too," he said quietly. "I haven't had a day off in a month. I'm tired."

"Oh." Feeling guilty, she slowed. She hadn't thought that he might need some time away.

"Here," he said, taking up the other end of the cloth, "I'll help." When they'd rolled it and stowed it in the bucket of supplies, he surprised her by reaching out. With one long brown finger, he touched her nose, then let his hand drift to her upper arm.

Again she stilled, surprised when he squeezed her arm, then began to stroke her from shoulder to wrist. Through the fabric of her long-sleeved shirt, she felt each of his strong fingers, felt the power in them that he used not to threaten, but to soothe and calm.

"It's all right, Lucy. We're just gonna talk, that's all. You have my word I won't touch you—not even with my hand on your arm like this. You'll be safe with me. Okay?"

She couldn't have moved if a charging bull came thundering at her. His tenderness trapped her far more than any amount of force. She felt caught in a golden lariat of yearning. How little gentle care she'd received in her life. How few times *anyone* had stroked her.

At that moment she was completely, totally helpless.

Rusty's caress didn't frighten her, she realized. And she so wanted to believe him. Would she be safe?

Before she could think, she murmured, "A day away would be nice. Yes, Rusty, I'll go on your picnic."

Chapter Five

Well, she'd wanted to improve her horsemanship skills, hadn't she? Swell idea. Lucy gripped the leather reins of her mount with both hands and hoped the rangy paint gelding which Rusty had saddled for her wouldn't bolt. Although the animal had yet to take a step, Lucy needed to force herself not to grip the horn. Only dudes did that.

Morning sunlight glinted off the water trough's still surface, threw short, boxy shadows from the barn onto the dirt. Everything this morning seemed too bright, too broad. Even the mount Rusty had assigned her stretched her legs and felt too big around.

She did love horses—always had—and she'd longed to get back in their company. Yet fifteen years ago, sitting on a gelding's back hadn't seemed to perch her so far off the ground. Back then she hadn't been so aware of her own physical vulnerability—her own mortality. Stiffly she held herself still and stared at the miles-away ground. It was hard-packed dirt, and she could see sharp little rocks down there, too. If she fell off, something was bound to break. An arm, a leg. Her neck.

"You all right?" Rusty asked, swinging easily into his own saddle. His coiled rope hung from a rawhide strap beside his thigh, and canvas saddlebags had been buckled over his sorrel gelding's rump. A black felt hat, faded denim shirt, worn jeans and roper boots completed the image of a working cowboy.

Her secret fantasy come to life: a man who worked the land so that his hands grew hard and tough, so that sun wrinkles bracketed his eyes, so that his gaze was clear, direct and honest. A cowboy.

Lucy marveled at the picture before her. A special magnetism surrounded Rusty. Even as a child, she'd felt it. Now in the prime of his life, his heroic, larger-than-life aura seemed more tangible, more powerful than ever.

The man could be a throwback to a time when cowhands had enjoyed their heyday; if she hadn't known he'd been a successful attorney, she would never have guessed.

Wrenching her thoughts back, she squared her shoulders. "Of course I'm all right," she replied haughtily. "Perfectly. I'm just a little…um, out of practice, that's all." With a surreptitious movement she was sure he didn't notice, she casually dropped her right hand from the reins and, as best she could, emulated his casual grip.

It was hard to relax. In the past twenty-four hours she'd almost canceled their picnic a thousand times. She shouldn't be alone with Rusty. *Alone with Rusty.* Just the idea made her think of things they might do together. Shared gazes, caught breaths, bodies brushing.

Alone.

Lucy bit her lip. Often he'd been curt with her, but yesterday he'd actually seemed to like her. Memory of the incredible pleasure his simple touch had evoked alarmed her all over again. Making her even more apprehensive was that she *wanted* to be close to him. Maybe she could still cry off. She darted a glance at the closed gate; it wasn't too late.

"Lucy." Rusty shifted in his saddle. "You sure you're all right?"

While she debated silently whether to stay in familiar territory or go with him into the unknown, she noticed a concerned frown pinch his brows together.

"You want to go...don't you, Lucy?" he asked quietly. The answer seemed important to him.

Trapped.

"Sure." She wasn't sure at all.

Guiding his horse to the corral gate, he leaned over and opened the latch without dismounting, then waited for her to urge her own horse through the fence opening. "You're out of practice, huh? How long's it been since you last rode?"

Remembering to squeeze her legs to make the animal go forward, Lucy got the horse through. "Quite a while, actually." She shrugged. "A number of years."

"Like...fifteen?"

Shooting him a suspicious glance, she saw the amused doubt in his eyes. "All right." She sighed wryly. "I haven't fooled you. The last time I rode was with you—behind your saddle." She wondered if he remembered.

They walked their horses in silence, the sturdy

hooves kicking up soft explosions of dirt as they headed for the ranch's picnic spot she knew was a mile or so into the meadow.

He said, "It was the afternoon we sat in the tree," and her heart warmed that he recalled the experience. The memory was important to her—a turning point in her life—albeit a sad one. But, for the teenaged boy he'd been, the day might seem like any other. How could it possibly hold the significance for him that it had for her?

"Your mom took you away the next morning," Rusty stated, surprising her again.

"Yes." After that day there'd been no more gentle country mornings in her life. No more horses snuffling along her sleeve for watermelon rinds, no more welcome scents of alfalfa and saddle leather. What followed was a sterile succession of cramped city apartments, impersonal boarding schools, then…Kenneth.

"Where did your mother move you? A time or two, I wondered."

Before he finished, she was already shaking her head. Those bitter memories had left a chilled place on her soul. Giving voice to them would only make the harsh cold bite deeper.

She pulled back emotionally. "Nowhere exciting. We lived in different cities. Rusty, what do you call that flower?" She pointed to a tiny yellow bloom close to the ground.

He frowned at her abrupt change of topic but didn't press her. "I call that a weed."

"Oh," she said, smiling a little. "I see. A weed."

"Yeah, but Landon knew the names of all the flowers. The trees, too. He had a real good memory for everything that grew around here."

"And Tom? What was he good at?" She pretended not to notice his stern expression that said, *You're avoiding the issue.*

"My brothers weren't around when you were here as a kid, were they? Well, Tom was good at winning rodeo buckles. He could rope the wind." His expression lightened. "Tom was a team roper—a heeler—and good enough to make it on the circuit. Never did try, though."

For someone to be skilled enough to become professional—at *anything*—and not do it, was to her, astonishing. "He was good enough, but didn't go? Why not?"

"Didn't want to travel so much." He looked at her from beneath the brim of his hat. "He liked it here."

She thought about life on the go, living out of a suitcase. It wasn't what she wanted—wasn't the life she was now trying to create for herself on the Lazy S.

From somewhere inside, a smile began forming before she even knew it. She felt it bubbling up from her heart, widening her mouth, spreading gladness to her eyes and cheeks. "I like it here, too," she told him with an unexpected gush of enthusiasm. "I *love* it here."

Somehow both horses came to a halt, and Rusty kept staring directly into her eyes. He searched for truth, she thought, shivering in the sunlit warmth. He was probing, assessing, measuring her for honesty. It seemed vitally important not to break the link of their gazes. Looking back, she met him levelly, let him see deep inside her.

Slowly his brown eyes heated, and instead of consciously holding his gaze, she was now held *by* it. She could feel his force of will working on her, seducing her. Lucy's mouth went dry. Alarm clanged inside her head. All at once she knew exactly what he was thinking.

"Rusty," she whispered, "you...you said you wouldn't touch me."

His eyes didn't flicker. If anything, they became a deeper shade of mahogany. "And have I?" His tone challenged her, dared her and tempted her, all at the same time.

"No, but..." At last she could lower her gaze, but heard his roughly in-drawn breath.

"I won't lie to you, Lucy. Guess it shows I want to. I want to touch you from your pretty, silky head down to your little feet. And everywhere in between."

She shook her head, denying him, wanting him.

"You're beautiful," he pressed. "And all woman. How much of a man would I be—living in the same house with a female like you and not want to feel you," he paused and his voice lowered, "not want to feel you beneath me?"

Stunned, she kept her head down.

His horse stamped a foot, and three barn swallows winged past.

"Please," she said belatedly, "don't say those things."

"Why not?" His voice was stark.

"Because, I can't— I...I don't—" Cutting herself off, she took a shallow breath and began again. "I didn't come to the Lazy S for that. I want a family, Rusty. Not a lover."

"*Family,*" he echoed in disbelief. "You mean, you want to treat me like some kind of...of brother?"

At least he understood, she thought, relieved. She nodded firmly. "Yes. A brother."

Surprising her, he threw back his head and guffawed.

"What's so funny?" She risked a glance at him, urging her horse forward. Both animals resumed their steady, swinging gait. Before then a clump of willows gave way to a small, still-green meadow. Sun drenched the circle of trees and foot-tall grass.

"Woman, I think maybe you've lost a few head of cattle from your herd." His laughter filled the fall air.

She sniffed, annoyed.

"There's nothing brotherly about the way I feel about you, Lucy," he stated emphatically, humor draining away as fast as it had come. "And you're lying if you say you think of *me* that way."

She opened her mouth to protest.

He dared her with a hard look.

Blinking rapidly, she glanced around for a diversion. "We're here, aren't we? Good. I'm famished. What's for lunch?" Reining her horse to an old wooden post sunk deep into the ground and fitted at the top with an iron ring, she prepared to dismount. Even with the short ride, she could feel her inner thigh muscles protest.

Rusty stopped her. "Lucy." He waited until she looked at him. "You're safe with me. You know that, don't you?"

She nodded, but was aware that her confusion showed. How was she to feel anything but apprehension after his bald admission that he wanted her?

By the time Lucy had her right leg over the saddle, Rusty was off his horse and on the ground beside her. As she dropped down, her feet touched solid earth. She was a bit sore, but the slight buckle in her knees surprised her. Flailing out, she caught at Rusty's arm—

already raised as if he knew she'd need his support. Through his shirt she could feel his forearm's corded muscles, his warm flesh.

In an instant she had her balance and let go, but swiftly surveyed his face.

Backing away, he raised his hands shoulder high, palms toward her. Humor lurked in his eyes. "Hey, don't give me that look—*Sis.* I didn't touch you, you touched *me,* remember?"

"I didn't say anything," she defended.

"Just keep your distance," he warned lightly, rooting out halters with lead ropes from his saddlebags. "I didn't ride out here to get seduced by the likes of you."

She flushed. "Oh, for Pete's sake—"

"I mean it now. Stay back. Don't try using your wiles on me." He laid a hand on his chest and lifted his chin. "I'm not that kind of man."

This last was said so primly, Lucy couldn't help chuckling. And she appreciated his attempt to lighten things between them. "I'll try to keep my hands off the merchandise," she said drily.

Glancing around, she took in the spot. Lovely old willows sheltered one side of the area, their drooping bows graceful and still green. Nevada-wild sage and a few tiny wildflowers were strewn about as if tossed by a carefree hand.

"Oh, Rusty, it's so beautiful." She sighed, helping him secure the horses. "Others should have the opportunity to enjoy this pastoral setting. When we begin guest ranching, I can just picture a small crowd of them here, happily—"

"Flicking lit cigarettes into the brush, starting wildfires," he finished for her. "Getting bogged down in the mud so we have to haul them out, getting lost so we have to go find them. You see a cheerful group, Lucy. I see a world of trouble when the government starts taxing the property as recreational. I see health regulations and costly permits and guys nosing around from Fish and Game—''

"All matters we can deal with." She waved her hand dismissively. Why was he always the voice of doom? Whenever she thought of the subject, she was filled with enthusiasm. "We aren't doing anything about it right now," she said by way of assuring him, "but there's no harm in discussing the possibilities, is there?"

He grunted, no reply at all, and turned to loosen cinches and unbuckle saddlebags.

"The bunkhouses are barely used," she said lightly, "what with so many of the hands married and in their own cottages. We could convert them into guest cabins. We could offer exercise classes, bring in someone to perform relaxing massages—''

"Massages!" he exclaimed, shuddering. "A masseuse—on a cattle ranch!" He shook his head. "I don't think you get it, Lucy. Most ranchers have what Hollywood calls 'rugged independence.' But I've often thought that term was really coined for men who typically don't like the general public. Their 'rugged independence' arises because they fight anything and everything that threatens their way of life. *That's* why they're ranchers. Most I know would sooner go belly-up than turn their property into dude getaways."

She thought about that. "Well...if that's so for them, I can see that. But you're different. You've lived in the city, worked in the corporate world, slaved in glass-enclosed, airless offices, fought rush-hour traffic. You *understand,* I know you do, what motivates me with this.''

He nodded. "Understand, yes. Accept?" He paused, choosing his words. "The idea of a careless public overrunning the place is abhorrent.''

The impasse between them loomed like a towering, unscalable wall. Their visions were totally at odds. Lucy stared at him pensively. Although she hadn't given up, she recognized that he, in turn, hadn't given an inch, either.

"Let's not push things today," Rusty suggested, holding out the lunch-filled saddlebags like a peace offering. "It's supposed to be a day off to relax. Let's take it easy.''

A reprieve, she thought, relieved they wouldn't have to argue, at least for a while. But deep inside, she felt it a crime to keep such a place secret. While respecting his opinion, she could not understand his attitude.

"Good idea," she agreed. "We've got months and months to work things out.''

After that, the tense air around them dissipated. On a tartan flannel blanket, Rusty laid out turkey sandwiches, quartered apples and lemon cookie bars Fritzy had baked. He reclined on one elbow while Lucy sat cross-legged. The new jeans she'd bought while in Reno were stiff, but her lace-up boots were comfortable. She wouldn't get her toes blistered, thank goodness.

When they'd eaten, Rusty casually asked about her father. She was amazed she was able to answer with comparative ease.

"My father?" She shrugged, swallowing a last apple slice. "I don't remember him. He left sometime when I was very small. My mother just said he was a louse, and she wouldn't answer my questions. Finally I gave up asking.''

He considered that for a moment. "The men in your life haven't treated you all that well?''

She shrugged again. "Bad luck, I guess.''

"It goes to figure,'' he concluded slowly, "that you wouldn't hold a lot of trust for them.''

"I like men,'' she stated.

"Didn't say that. Said you wouldn't be quick to trust a man.''

She had no notion how to reply, merely watched as a blue jay sailed by on an updrafting breeze.

"Lucy, I've got an idea of the kind of jerk your husband was. But you were married several years, weren't you? What I don't get is, why'd you stay with him? Why didn't you just pack up your bags and light out?''

There it was, that question she hated. Sooner or later, she'd known she would have to try and explain. She owed Rusty that much.

Yet, how did one recount in words a prison of emotional and psychological bonds, of despair vying against hope, a debilitating, learned helplessness which had kept her more thoroughly trapped than the stoutest iron bars?

"I was eighteen,'' she began on a breath so deep it almost hurt. "I wanted to get away from my mother. She had such strong opinions, Rusty. She was so opinionated and so—''

"Dominating?'' he cut in shrewdly. "I recall her ordering everyone around like a queen.''

Lucy acknowledged his point with pursed lips. "I met Kenneth at a small charity fund-raiser my mother dragged me to. He was older and very charming. We started dating, and I found him extremely attentive. He bought me gifts, wanted to hear about every aspect of my day like it fascinated him more than anything in the world. All that attention was flattering, and I welcomed it. A sophisticated, handsome, wealthy man wanted mousy little Lucy.'' She shook her head in wonder.

As if it tasted like dirt, Rusty set aside a half-eaten sandwich. "What went wrong?"

"I wish I'd had enough experience to realize all that attention wasn't healthy, wasn't normal. He…he changed. But the changes came gradually, so that it was hard to pinpoint exactly when. It started with comments that subtly put me down. He had a sort of witty sarcasm that could really cut, followed by hours or days of cool indifference.''

"Didn't you reason with him? Fight back?"

"I tried, but things got worse. He'd say, 'What's wrong with you—making a big deal out of nothing?'. He told me if I were more loving, a better wife, he'd be kind, so I tried overlooking things, tried being more understanding and undemanding. Pacifying him was incredibly difficult. I walked on eggshells, hoping not to set him off. But always after weeks of tension in our home, he'd have a big blowup. After his anger was spent, we'd have a wonderful period of harmony, and I'd have the old Kenneth back—the one I'd fallen in love with.''

Without a word Rusty shot to his feet and strode to the edge of a tiny stream that ran through the meadow. Stiff and tense, he stood there, staring down at the ribbons of water flowing over mossy rocks. She watched him but didn't move from her position on the blanket.

Hugging her knees to her chest, she wished the subject of her marriage had never come up.

Rusty kept staring at the water. "I still don't get it. If the bad times so often outweighed the good, why didn't you just pack up and leave?"

She rubbed her eyes. "I didn't recognize it then, but he kept me in a vicious cycle by making me doubt myself. I lost esteem without even realizing it. I learned to tolerate his behavior because I hoped so desperately he'd love me the way he did at first, treat me with consideration, with kindness. The trap developed when sometimes he actually would. Don't you see, Rusty? Few and far between as they were, I *lived* for those times."

At last a glimmer of comprehension began to show in his eyes. "Good God," he muttered harshly. "It sounds like hell."

"It was hell. He was so horribly jealous he'd wait outside restaurant ladies' rooms for me, imagining I was meeting some other man. When I'd go marketing, he'd check my car mileage—accuse me of rendez-vousing with someone. He called it a sign of his love. Over time I became so isolated—he didn't like my friends, didn't like my mother, so I saw them less and less, and finally, not at all." She looked at him bleakly. "He wouldn't even allow me credit cards or a check-book. Wealthy as he was, he parceled out dollar bills like they were gold nuggets, so most of the time I had no money."

Rusty grimaced and turned tensely back toward the water. Lucy saw his jaw working, but she was on a roll.

"Kenneth liked to wake me from a sound sleep—

mostly around midnight. You've already seen that I still have bad dreams—"

"Nightmares," he corrected harshly. "I don't want to hear any more, Lucy." Rusty whirled to face her, hands clenched into fists, features stony.

"You pushed me to tell you," she said, voice tight. Wrapping her arms about her middle, the pain and shame of remembered agony pulsed through her. "And you want to know why I stayed. But, you see, I was convinced if I couldn't relate to my husband, how could I get along in the world?"

"Bastard," he ground out. "A man who could treat a woman like that—treat *you* like that— I almost wish he were alive so I could go after him." For a moment Lucy saw the violent flashpoint of rage in Rusty's expression. While she knew it wasn't directed at her, she felt a moment's uneasiness.

Through the cloudy, crimson-tinged film of his fury, Rusty looked down at Lucy and read the subtle signs of her withdrawal: slim arms wrapped across her chest as if to hug herself, shoulders bowed inward. Her sudden wariness came through clearly in her widened eyes and her careful edging away from him. All at once he was disgusted with himself. He'd forced these admissions from her, and then gotten mad himself. Lucy needed gentle consideration, not another angry man.

At his sides his arms ached. It took all his will to keep rooted and not reach out for her. He longed to pull her to his chest, enfold her in tenderness and kiss away her memories of abuse. The urge to comfort her drummed through him so powerfully his hands shook. He thrust them into his front jeans pockets.

He'd made a promise: no touching. If there was a chance of winning even a small measure of trust from

Lucy, he must keep his word. And although he didn't really understand why it had become important, he knew that trust from her would be a priceless gift indeed. He wanted that.

"Maybe we ought to head back to the ranch," she suggested, surprising him. She melted farther away from him, eased toward the picnic blanket to gather leftover food into the saddlebags. He felt the loss keenly.

"Go back?" he echoed. "Yeah, sure. Guess we should." His voice sounded wooden. With jerky steps he went to the horses, tightened cinches and slipped on bridles.

On the ride back, little was said. A cloud of confused frustration enveloped him, made his head swirl with conflicting emotions. He wanted to keep Lucy close by his side, and conversely, to get as far away from her as possible. The push-pull made him unsettled and restless.

At ranch headquarters he brushed aside her offer to help put away the horses.

"Thank you for the picnic." At the barn crossties, she hovered uncertainly before him as he stripped their mounts of gear. "It was good to get a day off."

He nodded but didn't look at her. With efficient strokes he brushed the horses and wished she'd go up to the house. After a moment she turned and wandered away, carrying the blanket and leftover food. Knowing he was acting irrationally didn't help, because as soon as he heard the screen door bang behind her he wanted her back.

With a muttered curse he threw the brush into a bucket. Her need prodded him, aroused his protective instincts to rescue her from the pain of her past, show her how a real man treated a fine woman like her.

He didn't believe that Lucy was deliberately manipulative, but the effect on him was the same. Angry again and castigating himself, Rusty ground his teeth together. How sweet and nice and gooey he got around her.

"Damn."

He squinted out over the ranch, over *his* land. Roots of the meadow cottonwoods clawed deep for creek water. No rain had fallen yet, but the land bided its time with eternal patience. If one knew how to listen, the earth's rhythmic pulse could be felt, waiting.... Rusty listened. And he could feel it.

Still some green remained in the grass, and eager cattle cropped the tiny shoots to grow healthy and fat. There was wealth here, all manner of it.

He'd long known that on the northern section of the ranch, underground deposits of black gold pooled. Oil. It was time to get that acreage leased to a mining company, just as he had for the gypsum. Water rights for the many streams and creeks crossing the Lazy S were owned by the ranch—he planned to sell a percentage to his westerly neighbor for hay farming, as he had to the paint store owner.

Beatrice, up at the diner, had mentioned that a couple of sheepmen had stopped in asking about winter pasture for their stock. While sharing his fellow cattlemen's aversion to sheep, he knew the animal could be tolerated—and for the tidy profit they'd bring, tolerate them he would.

Turning the horses out, Rusty whacked his sorrel on the rump and watched it gallop off. Inside he felt, if not better, at least focused. He was as determined now

as he'd ever been to buy Lucy out by year's close.
Dude Ranch, my hind end. Just because he found her
physically attractive didn't change a thing.

For weeks after the picnic, Lucy barely saw Rusty.
Thanksgiving came and went with only a quiet meal
of baked ham, potatoes and green beans. Rusty bowed
his head to make a short blessing at the table thanking
the Higher Powers for Cricket, the child they all loved,
and asked for a mild winter. He ate everything on his
plate, thanked Fritzy and returned to work.

Even at subsequent dinners he spoke in monosyllables, gulped his food and found time only to play with
Cricket. Within ten or fifteen minutes he was heading
back out for a meeting with some stockman or other,
or to closet himself making phone calls or pore over
paperwork.

The harder he worked, the more Lucy worried. She
could see he'd stepped up his activity, and she supposed checks were coming in. She'd driven him away,
damaged his friendship by the sorry tale of her miserable marriage. It was all her fault. Bitterly, she regretted opening up to him. Why hadn't she kept her mouth
shut?

Another month passed, Cricket gained several
pounds and was now pulling herself up to stand pre-
cariously against table legs, bookshelves, even passing
ranch dogs who unfortunately refused to stand still.
More often than not, Cricket found herself plopping
onto her diapered bottom. Howling in complaint, she
would quickly crawl after and retry on any canine in-
attentive enough to stick around.

Her hair was growing, and the auburn down held

hints of someday becoming a luxurious sunset-hued mane.

Fascinated by the baby's almost daily changes, Lucy visited the library in the nearby town of Lovelock and checked out several child development books and spent evenings perusing them. It shocked her—this unexpected affection for the infant that wasn't even hers. Lucy, a woman who'd never hoped to mother a child, found mothering natural and fulfilling and even joyous. Each of Cricket's tiny advances thrilled Lucy, filled her with pride.

In Lovelock some civic-minded group had draped holiday banners of green and red across the street and bracketed store entryways with poinsettia pots. Christmas was coming. She shopped, careful to keep her gifts modest. She had no wish to offend anyone by extravagant spending.

Yet Rusty was remote and unreachable, a work-driven man. While she knew it was nearly impossible for him to amass the required sum, she sadly recognized one immutable fact: he would never quit trying. All his labor had one goal: to oust her off the Lazy S.

Seated on the davenport one afternoon after Cricket had finished her bottle, Lucy forced herself to face the painful possibilities. *Would* he be able to raise enough money? Would he really throw her out, like old paint cans and vegetable peelings on garbage day? Apprehension poured through her, filled her throat with a cruel, hard lump she could not swallow.

And what about Cricket? In her arms the baby chattered and gnawed through drool on Lucy's wrist. Something sharp sank into her skin. "Ouch," she cried, jerking her arm away.

Startled, Cricket gazed wide-eyed into Lucy's face.

"What's in your mouth, Cricket?" Lucy asked, bending over her. Thinking perhaps the baby had gotten hold of some toy, she pushed her fingers past the child's wet lips and felt a hard ridge on her upper gums. Peering inside, Lucy saw two tiny squares of white. "Why, my goodness, you've got teeth!"

Cricket drooled down her shirtfront, grinning as if proudly showing off. Lucy clapped her hands and duly admired her new smile, although she knew the baby couldn't possibly be aware of such a detail in her growing body.

Cloaking the child with her arms, Lucy hugged her tight. Lovely scents of baby powder and shampoo wafted up. Plump skin felt velvety and precious. She closed her eyes, savoring the moment.

It didn't seem likely, but she was forced to admit it was possible Rusty might succeed. And if he did, would she find herself torn away from everything important in her life? Would she find herself adrift and alone…again?

Without admitting it, even to himself, Rusty sought out the one person he knew would offer him sound advice.

"Beatrice," he began, after wasting a good thirty minutes chewing the fat with old Jim Curlan and eating a tuna melt he didn't want, "sit down for a minute. Tell me about everything going on with you."

The waitress eyed him suspiciously, but slid onto the next stool. In the window behind her, a neon sign flashed the name of a popular soda. "You want to hear about me? That's a first. What's on your mind, Rus?"

She smiled in expectation, and he was annoyed she saw through him so easily. This late in the afternoon the diner was nearly empty, with the supper crowd not due to descend for another two hours, so being overheard didn't concern him. Yet it was tough for him, soliciting another's opinion when he ought to be man enough to figure things out on his own.

But he was at a loss.

From the remains of his late lunch he picked up a bread crust and ate it. Then he selected a cold French fry and ate that, too. Beside him, Beatrice waited.

When he began to seriously consider picking up the wilted lettuce leaf, she asked shrewdly, "How's that little gal up at your place, Rus? Lucy, isn't it?"

He shot her a glance, surprised and yet not surprised she could put her finger on the wound so quickly. "Fine," he said, frowning. "Just great. Really. She's...fine."

He could feel Beatrice's concerned gaze study his profile. "You like her," she said. "A lot. I know that. I've been around enough to tell."

He said nothing, yet could feel an uncomfortable flush rise up his neck. Hell, he thought, disgusted. He was too old for this.

"So...does she like you?"

"What? Sure. Why wouldn't she?" The conversation was getting ridiculous. He didn't like Bea's probing, and yet he'd come here specifically to talk to her about this. His mood began to sour.

Beatrice pursed her carmined lips. "Bring her in here. I'd like to meet her. The boys from your place have been talking about her. They like Lucy, say she's real sweet—patches up their wounds and takes good care of Tom's baby."

Reluctantly Rusty nodded. "Lucy's good with the

baby. And she's easy to get along with. Easy on the eyes, too," he added as an afterthought.

"Dang it, Rusty Sheffield," Beatrice spat out, "why don't you admit you're crazy about her? It's as plain as that hat on your head—which I'd appreciate your taking off when you come into my diner. Just say it, it won't hurt."

"Bea, mind your own damn..." He'd run fresh out of righteous steam before he could even finish. His own sense of fairness wouldn't allow him to attack Bea for what he'd wanted from her in the first place. He rubbed his forehead, doffed his hat and set it crown-side down on the counter. "Truth is—" he drew a difficult breath "—around Lucy I feel weak as a dragged cat."

There, it was out.

"That wasn't so hard, now was it?" She scoffed at him. "So, what's the problem?"

"We're in business together," he tried explaining. "I never asked for her to come around and invest in the Lazy S. I didn't want to sell half my land."

"That's a done deal—in the past." She waved that off. "Why are you whining about it now?"

He cast her a baleful glance. "She wants to make the place into a dude ranch, with yoga classes and swimming pools and, I don't know, bird watchers—"

"Dude ranch!" Beatrice reared back on her stool, and her thin eyebrows shot up. "Whoa. Where'd she get a half-baked idea like that?"

He shrugged grumpily. "Lucy liked the place as a kid, says more people should 'experience the peaceful country.' He rolled his eyes. "She's got it in her head that we should share the 'pastoral setting' with stressed-out city folk."

"Oh." Bea thought about that.

"See what I mean?"

"Well, this truly is God's country," she said proudly. "Why anyone would want to live anywhere else—"

"*Bea,*" he said, stalling her with an upraised hand, "for once I need you on my side."

She lifted one shoulder. "I am, dear. Still, nothing you're saying seems too serious. If you really like Lucy, you can talk to her, work things out between you."

Shaking his head before she was through, Rusty began to feel worse. He shoved his plate away. "Not possible. What she wants and what I want are miles apart."

Drumming her fingers on the counter, Bea gazed at him pitifully. "You really can't be this dense, can you? But then, you *are* of the male persuasion." She said *male* like it was a dirty word. "I swear, if you had another brain, it'd be lonely."

He got to his feet, fished bills from his jeans and tossed them on the counter. "Thanks a lot."

She threw up her hands. "I know you're a good man, Rusty, so I won't lose all faith. Why don't you ask Lucy for a date? You could bring her in here."

"A date?" He liked Beatrice and knew she meant well. But this time she was way off the mark. Carefully he explained, "Lucy's my business partner. I don't want to date her."

"Yes, you do," the obstinate woman retorted.

Rusty mustered his most threatening scowl and pushed his face intimidatingly close to hers. "No, I don't."

Completely unfazed as usual, she thrust her own face

an audacious inch closer. Nose to nose, she enunciated, "Yes…you…do!"

Grabbing his hat, Rusty walked out, doggedly shaking his head. It had been a mistake, discussing his private concerns with Beatrice. But no harm was done. Although she'd tried persuading him all would be well, he was now more convinced than ever that the problems between Lucy and him were truly insurmountable. As he'd stated, there could be no middle ground.

Date Lucy. He rolled his eyes at the moronic suggestion. Huh. Not in this lifetime.

Chapter Six

Lucy fretted the next afternoon away, barely picked at the savory meat loaf supper Fritzy had cooked, and by eight o'clock that night she could stand it no more. Cricket had long since been tucked into bed, and Rusty had raced out right after clearing his plate to tend a colicky horse.

Tossing aside a thick, hard-backed library book titled, *Zoom! Life in the Fast Lane, Your Baby's First Year,* Lucy shot to her feet.

"I'm going down to the barn," she announced to Fritzy, a completely useless exercise since Fritzy paid little attention to Lucy's comings and goings, and now barely looked up from her embroidery of some fleecy red fabric. "To find Rusty," Lucy added unnecessarily.

"That's nice," Fritzy replied absently. Her gray topknot slipped to one side as she bent over a particularly difficult stitch.

"All right, then. I'll just…go now." Lucy heard her own voice and wondered at herself. Why did she feel the need to proclaim her intentions tonight? Apprehension did strange things to people, she guessed, yanking on a heavy sheepskin coat she found on the hall tree. With winter's onset, the nights had become bitterly cold, and she was grateful for the oversize coat's fleecy lining. Not bothering to button it up, she left the edges hanging open.

Outside, she tucked her chin down against the chill and hurried toward the spill of soft apricot light beckoning from the barn's half-opened doorway. Beneath her tennis shoes, gravel crunched. The small disturbance made an oddly anxious noise, Lucy decided ruefully—if her mind could make sound, her troubled thoughts would probably have the discordant pitch of rocks crushed together.

Slipping inside, she followed the low rumble of Rusty's voice, past rows of neatly hung saddles, Indian-print blankets, halters and bridles. He was alone in the great barn.

She hadn't expected that. She'd figured the veterinarian, or at least a few cowhands would be hanging around, solemnly debating doctoring techniques or just shooting the breeze. Swallowing hard, she decided this was best, since she needed her questions answered in private, anyway.

"You'll be fine," he was murmuring at the barn's other end, beyond a towering stack of fragrant baled hay. "Sure you will, girl. Just relax. That's it. Take it easy." And on he went. Lucy found him at the back of the last stall, stroking the neck of a handsome ebony mare. When she peered over the stall door, he glanced up. His boots were half-buried in clean shavings, and stems of alfalfa clung to his shirt. Even at this late hour he still wore his black hat.

Lucy nodded at the mare. "How is she doing?"

"Better. The guys have taken turns walking her for hours—the usual treatment. I sent them all off to get some rest. I can watch her now."

"I see," she said. "Um, will she be okay?"

"I've just got to make sure she doesn't lie down. I don't think she will now, but she's still kicking up her hind leg toward her stomach."

"Why is she doing that?" Lucy unlatched the stall door and approached slowly. Now that she was here, she didn't quite know how to get the information she wanted. Yet it was vitally important that she do so. The uncertainty of her position was going to drive her crazy. She put her hand on the mare's soft muzzle.

"Colic is just a horse bellyache," Rusty answered. "They can get it different ways—bad hay, drinking water that's too cold—things like that. The trouble comes when it isn't taken care of properly. It can kill a horse in hours."

Lucy said soberly, "I didn't know colic was so serious."

"It's not always." He patted the animal's neck. "But we can't afford to lose Matilda. She's only ten, and she's been a great brood mare. Turned out several good colts for me. She's gentle, too."

"You really like her, don't you?"

"Sure." He threw Lucy a faintly surprised glance. "I like all the horses."

"And..." She bit her lip, fiddling with the mare's untrimmed whiskers. "You want lots more colts out of Matilda, for lots more years, so the ranch has a good supply of cow horses, right?"

"Right." If his frankly questioning brows were any indication, he was wondering why she kept stating the obvious. Expectation wavered in the air like dust motes.

Struggling for poise, Lucy searched for the right words to elicit his intentions, should he reach his financial goal by year's end. Had anything changed in his thinking? Would he allow her to stay?

He was still waiting for her to explain herself, but the words wouldn't come. Suddenly miserable, she felt her mouth begin to tremble. It was getting harder by the second to fight down her growing dread.

"I really like the horses, too," she managed. "And the men. They're all so nice. And, of course, Fritzy." She stopped, then rushed on. "And Cricket—she's a doll. I'm crazy about her, you know. And...and she's getting attached to me, too, I think."

She scanned his face, hoping he'd see where she was going.

All she found was a puzzled frown.

Hell, she was muddling this terribly. Why couldn't she express herself? Why couldn't she just spit it out?

Because his answer would decide her entire future? Because she knew her heart would expand or shrivel depending on what he might say?

Lucy realized she was staring at Rusty in mute appeal. She must look like a forlorn child, she thought in disgust. All big eyes, wobbly lips and awkward, incomprehensible statements. How pathetic. How embarrassing.

With that thought she lost her nerve. Swinging around on her heel, she reached for the latch. "Well. I'm glad the mare is okay. Going back to the house now." In six quick steps, she was out of the stall and headed for the barn door when Rusty called out.

"Lucy, wait."

She halted, peered back over her shoulder. This had been a bad idea from the get-go. "Yes?" A painfully mortifying blush crept up her neck; she could feel the heat spread across her cheeks. He must think her a blithering idiot. Lord, she had to get out of there.

He followed her, shutting the stall behind him. Walking right up to her, he left mere inches between them. Hastily she retreated a step, but he closed the gap until her back came up flush against the haystack. He was so tall she was forced to tilt back her head to meet his gaze.

The wall lamp's dim wattage limned the brim of his hat, the edge of his jaw, formed hollows in his clean-shaven cheeks. His brown eyes gleamed as he assessed her. "That coat," he nodded at the sheepskin. "It's mine."

"Oh." If there had been any room between them she would have spread her hands. As it was she could only swallow nervously. "I just grabbed it off the hall tree. Are you cold? Do you want to wear it now?"

As she made to tear it off, he stopped her. "No, I don't want it now. I'm used to the cold." The force of his masculine energy buffeted her like wind over the prairie. "I think it looks damn good on you, that's all."

At his compliment, a tiny thrill shot through her. "It's too big," she muttered.

"We ought to get you one in your size." With his calloused hands, he reached out to turn up the collar at her nape. Ever so gently, his fingers grazed the back of her neck, then skimmed around to raise the white fleece beside her ears. "Until then you're welcome to wear my coat anytime. Keep the collar up, and you'll be warmer. And button it down the front."

Sliding his hands from the collar to the thick front

placket, he brought the edges together. She dropped her chin and watched, fascinated, as degree by degree his work-roughened fingers trailed lower. The slow gliding movement struck Lucy as sensual. In fact, everything about him did. It could be his expression, his mouth relaxed, but for a small, rakish grin, his eyes half-closed and shooting sparks of sexual promise. Even his hat was tilted on a dashing angle.

Because the top button hit her rather low, his knuckles brushed against Lucy's upper chest. The room tipped crazily, and then her entire world ground to a halt. She went completely still. Even through the heavy garment, the shock of his fingers so close to her breasts robbed her of air.

All the moisture in her mouth dried and her breathing started up again in a shallow gasp. Not for anything could she have made a single move. Her mind whirled back to the afternoon before their picnic, when Rusty had stroked her arm and she had become immobilized with pleasure.

This was why she couldn't have him touching her—this hungry aching—this powerful reaction to his hands on her body—this terrible wanting that incapacitated her. Never in her life had she reacted to any man in such a manner.

She had always thought she'd loved Kenneth, but when he'd reached for her, not once had molten liquid seared through her body's veins and arteries like rivers of melted gold. Never had she truly *wanted* Kenneth. Not in the weak-kneed, mind-numbing manner in which she desperately wanted Rusty. She knew that now with crystalline clarity.

Exactly when he started pulling her toward him, inch by inch, using the upper edges of the coat, Lucy couldn't pinpoint. She knew only that inch by inexorable inch, she went willingly.

"On second thought," he told her, his gaze drifting to her lips, "maybe I am getting cold. Wish I could climb right into this coat with you. Get close. Real close."

"Oh," she said succinctly. "Oh."

"Maybe even skin to skin."

Her reply sounded strangled, completely inarticulate, even to herself.

"You smell good," he whispered, actually inhaling her until his nostrils flared. "Sweet and soft."

"So do you—smell good—that is. Horses," she whispered back in halting words. "Hay. Soap." Their bodies came up flush now. Lucy was acutely aware of his denim jeans scraping hers, his chest lightly resting against hers. The hay bales stacked high at her back and the wall at her side formed a sort of cage that Rusty closed with his body. It made a deliciously seductive snare that left her helpless to escape.

Lifting a hand to her hair, he threaded his fingers through the silky strands. "Tell me it's all right to touch you now, Lucy," he demanded huskily.

How she adored his caress. For the space of a heartbeat she closed her eyes and reveled in the pleasure rippling down her spine.

"I'm not breaking any promise, am I? I kept my word before."

"Yes." The word soughed from her.

"Then say it's all right now." His whisper was stark, with a strange compelling urgency she'd never heard from him before. With his fists on the coat beneath her chin, he drew her closer still, so his breath feathered gently over her lips. And then he stopped, waiting. A heavy, pulsing beat of anticipation passed, then another.

She knew he was asking to kiss her. He wasn't going to, unless she gave her consent. It thrilled her...that he was leaving all the power in her hands. He wanted to kiss her, and, Lord knew, she wanted him to.

It was wrong, an awful idea, and later she would count the cost in the breaking of her heart.

"Yes, please," she got out on a croak.

He smiled. With one hand at the back of her head and the other still holding the coat's edge beneath her chin, Rusty gathered her to him like the most precious gift. The tender impact of his mouth settling on hers hurled a jolt of electricity through her. Desire swept in delicious spirals outward from a spot deep in her chest.

She melted.

This had been impossible to avoid, inevitable. The thought tantalized her before a foglike sensuality enveloped her every sense. She'd known, but hadn't wanted to admit even to herself that the simmering attraction between them would eventually come boiling to the surface.

Rusty lightly rubbed his lips over hers. They were firm, warm, pliable. Perfect.

"Sweet," he muttered against her skin. "So sweet and right."

Right? The word echoed in her mind. What could he mean by that? When he deepened the kiss, slanted his mouth over hers, the new intimacy drove all other thoughts away. He dragged his tongue along her teeth in an erotic glide, then used it to probe deeper into her mouth.

Letting go of the coat, he cupped her cheek, then wrapped his other arm around her waist. His hand pressed subtly against her lower back, settled her into the intimate niche of his thighs.

She gasped again. That Rusty wanted her, he'd told her before. But the reality of his iron hardness pushing against her left her senses reeling. A wild desperation seized her. He'd said this was right. Nothing in the entire universe had ever been so right.

Hampered by the constricting coat, she could only lift her arms as high as his waist and grab hold of his leather belt. He was kissing her thoroughly now, but she could feel the strict control he exerted to keep the caress gentle. She shivered, loving the tenderness, and then felt a fine tremor in his palm cupping her face.

He was trembling—just as she was—Lucy thought in wonder. The knowledge of her own feminine power quivered through her. The therapist had been right, she recognized it now. Rusty seemed aroused...plenty! There was nothing wrong with her ability to interest a male. Gratitude spilled through her, and the awareness enriched her own arousal.

"Lucy," he muttered against her lips, "sweetheart, take off the coat."

She opened her eyes and blinked, still caught in a sensual haze. "It's warm in here, isn't it?" she asked thickly. "Very warm."

His smile was a flash of white. "Not warm, Lucy. Hot." He was already busy unfastening the single button he'd managed to secure and sliding the coat off her shoulders to toss it aside.

Without the garment, she suddenly felt stripped of an important barrier; she felt almost naked. It was silly, they both were fully dressed. And yet, when he faced her again, she couldn't meet his eyes.

Using the edge of his hand, he tipped her chin up.

"I want to touch you tonight, sweetheart. I want to feel you against me without any coat between us."

Struck shy, she couldn't look at him.

He dropped his hand, but remained close. His body was a substantial wall of masculine sinew, bone and muscle, an effective contrast to her small feminine softness. Never was she more aware of their fundamental physical differences, of the *rightness* of a man and a woman...together. "I know you haven't had a lot of kindness from men," he said. "But I promise not to hurt you in any way. Could you trust me this once?"

"Trust you to...do what?" She loathed how her voice faltered.

Slowly his gaze traveled down her chest, lingered there, at her waist, and lower. It felt like a burning brand. "I've been ignoring it, been fighting what's between us. But right now I can't. Can you?"

She tried to shrug casually.

The sound of a stamping hoof came from Matilda's stall. "I've got to check on the mare," he said reluctantly. "Come with me." Not waiting for her answer, he turned and walked to the end stall. He slipped inside, and she heard him murmuring to the animal.

For a long moment she wavered. With Rusty, she was too open, too defenseless. Too vulnerable. Eating at her was the tense knowledge that if she allowed further intimacies between them, things would change. And possibly not for the better. *Get out of here,* a voice warned. *Get out while you can.*

Instead, cautiously, she walked forward. When she reached the stall, he was already out, closing the door behind him.

"She'll be all right now," he said. "I'll look in on her later, just to be sure."

"I'm glad she's okay."

With indolent cowboy grace, he leaned back against the stall and propped one booted foot behind him. Using his thumb, he nudged back his hat and looked at her. "Come here," he invited.

"I...I ought to get back to the house."

"Your choice," he said. "I'd never force anything on you. If you'd rather go back and watch a little boring TV, fine by me. I won't stop you."

She nodded, understanding that he was offering her the option. Nerves jangling with misgivings, she darted a glance over her shoulder at the open doorway.

His eyes narrowed. "That's not how I want it, though. I want you here." He pointed to the spot in front of him and spoke with determined emphasis. "In my arms. I want to be kissing you and have you kissing me back. I want to put my hands on you, Lucy, and feel yours on me."

Shocked at hearing all this put into words, Lucy felt her eyes widen. Rusty had barely spoken to her these past weeks. She hadn't known he'd been fighting his attraction to her—just as she had to him. She didn't know his emotions ran so deep. A new, excited bud of elation began to unfurl within her.

He said, "I won't ask if you want that, too. I'll just leave things up to you." He paused, and his voice lowered to a hard command. "Go on back to the house, Lucy. Or come here. Come here and kiss me."

Good as his word, he didn't move toward her. She almost wished he would take matters from her, as he had moments ago during their first kiss. Then, he'd caught her by surprise. Clearly now he wanted it understood that she would be a willing participant.

He was being so careful, she thought. Probably more

so than he'd ever been with a woman. His disarming admission helped build her confidence. Here was the boy who'd sat with her in the meadow tree, the boy who'd climbed to comfort her. Rusty was all grown-up now, magnificently so, but that compassionate boy was still a part of him. Her reservations faded and the warnings from within stilled. How sweet he was, she decided. How romantic.

"There's hay on your shirt," she told him.

Frowning, he glanced at his shoulder, but left his arms at his sides. "So, take it off."

Her tennis shoe scraped against a pebble as she shuffled a single step closer. Rusty was a gorgeous, healthy male—a breath of clean fresh air in her life. "I will, Rusty," she said softly, smiling. "I want to."

Both knew she wasn't referring to the alfalfa.

Lifting her arms to twine around his neck, she forgot about the hay and sank into him. Their mouths met. Bodies merged, limbs wound sinuously about each other. Rusty's hat tumbled off, but Lucy barely noticed.

She moaned, enthralled by his hard warmth, by the rasp of his stubbled cheek. All her life she'd longed for him. The sound she made seemed to electrify him, and his arms crushed her closer still.

Rusty clamped her to him and could barely believe his luck. Lucy—so responsive, so delicately eager. How easy it was to put aside all his fine principles, to forget his talk with Beatrice. "I don't want to date Lucy," he'd declared indignantly.

No, he just wanted to hold her, kiss her silly, carry her straight to his bed and explore every inch of her fragrant flesh.

Who did he think he was fooling?

A moment ago it had taken all his discipline not to

grab her and kiss her again, but to give her the choice. If he hadn't, she might have responded to him as she had before, but something inside nagged: was she simply allowing his embrace, or did she actively want it? Call it a small test, but as he reveled in the imprint of her arms, breasts, mouth and belly—all transferring female body heat to him like a blowtorch—he had his answer.

This woman would burn him alive.

As if she couldn't get close enough, she curved one foot around his calf, and pressed her rounded breasts to him. Through her thin oxford shirt he could feel her tightly budded nipples. It had been a great idea to get that damned coat off her. If his mouth hadn't been otherwise occupied, he might have grinned in sheer masculine pleasure.

Who would have guessed? Little Lucy was a sexy she-cat.

He could feel her knees wobbling—nature's enticement to the female to lie down and accept her mate. As driving excitement pounded every available ounce of blood to his groin, he steadied her. She was ready for him, he thought in triumph. She wanted him in the most elemental way a woman could want a man. Right then he was completely certain he could do anything he pleased with her, and she would not protest.

The aching throb below his belt buckle increased. He'd desired Lucy from the first day she'd arrived on his ranch, and matters had only gotten worse. Now he had a chance to ease some of that. He could find release with her, then get on with other things.

As he lifted his mouth for air, Lucy mewled in protest, pressed her lips to his neck, pecked tiny, feminine kisses along the line of his jaw. She was such a slim woman, he marveled, so small and utterly female.

And trusting.

He'd asked her to trust him, vowed he wouldn't hurt her. Yet he knew without doubt that if he were to make love to her here, in the dusty barn, the experience would hurt her. Not physically, but emotionally. Even intellectually. Trust would be broken.

So what, he thought inwardly? She was a grown woman. There was nothing to stop two consenting adults from enjoying each other. Fiercely battling his doubts, he enclosed her tighter still.

At that moment she twisted away.

"*Stop,*" she rasped out, wrenching free of his arms to come to a stumbling halt just past the hay stack. Even in the uneven light he could see she was trembling head to foot; panic flashed in her eyes. "I...I can't." She put a hand to her lips. "You don't want me, Rusty."

"Yes, I—"

"No, not really. For tonight, yes. But that's all. Not for good."

He stared at her and ground his teeth in frustration. His body hammered at him to yank her close again, convince her with his mouth, his body, the strength of his desire, to acquiesce to him.

She was already moving toward the door.

"Lucy. Don't go."

Her shoulders curved forward, arms crossed and hands cupped over her elbows, she paused at the door and shot him a glance. It may have been the shadowy lighting, but her face appeared pale; her eyes were dark, wounded. He'd seen that anguished look once, in the eyes of a trapped bobcat.

"You know this is no good, Rusty. If I have to leave at the end of the year things will be awkward between us. And I, for one, won't feel good about myself."

He averted his face, conscience smiting him.

"I'm not holding you solely responsible for what happened tonight," she said, her chin lifting proudly. "I'm as much to blame."

His features twisted. "Blame? Nobody's to *blame* for God's sake."

"So, let's keep matters friendly," she went on doggedly. "But that's all." Her back firmed as she drew herself up. He could feel her withdrawing from him even further. How he hated when she did that. "Good night, Rusty."

For a long second she hesitated, her gaze a cool challenge. It seemed like she was waiting for him to say something, but what?

When he said nothing, she disappeared into the night. With a muttered imprecation he gave a wooden barrel of horseshoes a savage kick. The pain in his foot barely registered. What had she wanted him to do—promise her the moon and stars? Throw his entire life, his ranch—his *heritage* at her feet—a woman he was really only coming to know?

And for what?

"It's just a toss in the hay," he muttered, trying hard to convince himself.

Grimacing, he collected his hat, checked the mare a last time and secured the barn for the night with a slam of the heavy sliding door. Stomping outside, he glared at the full moon. It shone down, creamy and serene, its rays benevolent. Crickets sang out, and in a nearby pasture a cow bawled to her calf. All was calm.

Rusty realized that his shoulders were rigid and

cramped with tension, his jaw was working painfully.
What the hell was wrong with him? Thwarted physical
desire had never killed him before; in his youth there'd
been women who'd turned him down. So why, just
because she wanted only to be "friendly," was he fu-
rious to the point of violence? Why did he want to
break something, howl at the moon, curse at the top of
his lungs?

*Because she wasn't just any woman. Because she
was* Lucy.

Jerking off his hat, he stabbed stiff fingers through
his hair. He was angry, and maybe even a little confused. Things weren't right, by damn, and that irritated
and annoyed him, like a barbwire cut that wouldn't
heal.

It was a helluva problem—living with Lucy—wanting her but knowing she was off-limits. He scowled
into the black recesses of his hat, but he couldn't answer the final question badgering him.

Why did he keep remembering the bruised pain in
her eyes just before she'd walked out, and the way it
made him ache?

Chapter Seven

In the end Rusty forced himself to ask Lucy for a date, just as Beatrice had suggested, yet even as he did so, he could hardly credit it. Dating Lucy made no sense.

In the entry hall early the next morning, when winter's cool sunshine leaked in through the open front door, he stopped her. She wore a coat—not his sheepskin, he noticed—and she was juggling a bundled-up Cricket. It was apparent they were going for a walk.

Because he didn't want to see the creeping wariness in her eyes, he phrased it as if she ought to meet a few of the local people. "Since you're living here now," he remarked casually, "I thought you'd like to go up to Beatrice's Diner. You'll like Bea—she's a kick."

As expected, her brows drew cautiously together, but he thought he saw a flash of vulnerability in her eyes. She slid him a sidelong glance and, like Beatrice, saw through him like clear glass. "You're asking me out for dinner? For a date?"

He'd have to work on this troubling transparency, he

thought. Something told him to play things down, so he lifted a shoulder. "An early supper. No big deal." Very seldom in his life had he had occasion to attempt an innocent mien, and so his skill was iffy at best. But he tried now, scanning the ceiling tiles absently as if her answer meant nothing either way. All he knew was that he wanted to be with Lucy away from the ranch. He wanted her in his truck, with the white-lined pavement streaking past and her warmth snuggled up against him in the darkened cab.

As long as he stayed focused on the moment, and didn't think about what might or might not come about at year's end, he was all right.

"I...uh, don't know. What time did you have in mind?" she hedged, fidgeted with Cricket, and he could see she was casting around for some excuse—anything—to decline. As if the time of day would matter.

"You come with me, Lucy," he commanded, all at once tired of his own subterfuge. "I want you to come. Be ready at five."

"Oh, but what should I wear?" She hoisted a sliding Cricket back up onto her hip. He knew the baby was getting heavier all the time.

"Wear? Hell, I don't know," he responded automatically. "Whatever you wa—" The uncertain expression on her face stopped him. To him, she'd look good wrapped in a horse blanket, but he guessed that sort of thing would be important to a woman. Scratching his jaw, he tried to ponder the ins and outs of women's fripperies, yet the subject was beyond him. At last he awkwardly proclaimed, "What you're wearing now is fine."

She glanced down at herself in surprise. "Tennis shoes, jeans and a T-shirt?"

"Yeah. Fine." Pulling his hat low, he tweaked Cricket's nose, which earned a squeal of appreciation, and moved to brush past the woman and baby on his way to the office. Enough about clothes already, he had work to do. Besides, he'd achieved his objective: Lucy's agreement to the date.

"Rusty?" she said, and he swung to face her. "Fritzy can watch Cricket. I'll be ready at five."

It wasn't her statement that gave him pause, but her small, shy smile. He felt like smiling back suddenly, and didn't resist the impulse. Lucy liked him, he thought, even though at times he'd been tough on her. His steps felt light and airy. It was a great day to be alive.

Lucy really did like him.

Beatrice's diner was straight out of a fifties movie, Lucy thought, as Rusty ushered her through the glass door, on which hung a tinkling bell that heralded their arrival. Propped beside an ancient filling station advertising a flying horse as its logo, Beatrice's place seemed truly out of another time. If James Dean himself were leaning on the stool-fronted Formica counter, a cigarette drooping from his lower lip and his expression exuding indolent sensuality, she wouldn't have been surprised.

Red tin signs advertising soda pop hung on whitewashed walls next to a six-foot span of steer horns and handmade macramé designs. Small, twenty-five-cent jukeboxes topped each booth of teal vinyl seats, and sawdust actually covered the floor. Patrons half filled the diner: casually dressed cowboys in mud-clumped boots, families with two and three kids, and a few teen-agers.

A concession to the fast-approaching holidays, an enormous pinecone-dotted wreath hung behind the counter and scented the room with fresh evergreen. On each table holly cuttings tied with red velvet bows rested cheerily in green-tinted vases.

A florid woman sporting a brassy blond beehive and crimson lipstick bustled toward them. She carried an empty decanter of coffee. "Rusty," she exclaimed, "it's great to see you!"

He mumbled a hello as the woman turned to beam at Lucy. "Howdy," she trilled. "Howdy." She stationed herself squarely in their path, grinning expectantly at Rusty.

"Lucy, this is Beatrice," he got out. "She owns the place."

Beatrice scrubbed her hand on her apron and thrust it forward. Her long fingernails were painted the same hue as her lipstick. "Pleased to meet you, dear," she said. "Do sit down. You'll have supper, won't you? I do a lot of the cooking here, but I got a chef—Chang—some two years back who's a whiz in the kitchen. Now, I recommend the blue-plate special." She led the way to an empty booth like a proud parade marshal leading a marching band. "This here's my best table, Lucy. I'm so glad you could come."

"It's nice to meet you," Lucy said, at a loss. As she slid across the teal vinyl she noticed that Rusty looked distinctly uncomfortable. It appeared that the woman had known Lucy would be arriving, but she couldn't imagine how. Had Rusty discussed her with Beatrice?

"How about some coffee, dear?" Beatrice asked Lucy. "It's real strong, but good, right, Rusty?"

"Thick as oil," he muttered. "Tastes like creosote," he added, but she clearly wasn't listening.

"I'll grab menus," Beatrice called, hustling away, but she was back in seconds to hand them cracked plastic menus and to place a mug filled with steaming brew before Lucy. "Just take your time deciding," she suggested. "It don't have to be the blue-plate. Chang'll make anything your little heart desires."

Rusty cleared his throat. "How about some coffee for me?"

Beatrice blinked at him, frowning, as if he'd interrupted her in the middle of a vitally important conference. "Well, I don't have three arms, now do I, Rus? Lucy, do you take milk and sugar?"

Lucy smiled, feeling as if an unexpected gale had swept her into the heart of an amiable whirlwind. "I'd love some. Your place is so—" she glanced around "—so comfortable. I feel right at home, like I've been here a million times."

Beatrice straightened and positively glowed. "You're just too nice." Off she went.

"She's so friendly," Lucy observed. "No wonder people come here."

"There isn't much competition." Opening his menu, he stared into it and frowned.

"Here you are." Beatrice was already back, depositing a tiny pitcher, sugar bowl and a spoon before Lucy. "Normally we use milk in these little pitchers, but I found some fresh cream in the fridge."

"You didn't have to go to that much trouble," Lucy protested.

"No trouble, none at all. I'll be back in two shakes to take your order."

"Bea?" Rusty urged, "Some brew, please?"

Beatrice swiveled her head around to stare at him as if he'd just arrived. "My stars, but you men get more demanding every day. Rusty Sheffield, you've been comin' in here for fifteen long years—issuing orders like somebody voted you president. Lucy, have you ever seen the like?" As she leaned toward Lucy, her tone became woman-to-woman confidential. "It's a wonder we put up with 'em, isn't it?" She sighed sadly, shaking her head at him as if he were a dog that needed putting out. "Oh, well. I always say that if a man can't make you miserable, he can't make you happy, either."

Giggling, Lucy hid her face behind her mug as the woman disappeared.

"I don't know what it is," Rusty complained, "but everybody here always gets coffee, terrible as it is. But I never do."

Lucy laughed openly. "Could it be your sparkling personality?"

He grunted, making her laugh more, because she could see the underlying affection between the two. She really did feel at home in the diner, and she liked Beatrice and her plain-spoken manner. She couldn't help thinking that Beatrice was the kind of woman Kenneth would have instantly disliked. Bea was too confident. Too opinionated. He would have called her "common," although not publicly. In his superior fashion, he would have whispered the insult in Lucy's ear, while treating Beatrice courteously, but coldly.

A quick veil of melancholy swathed her heart. Kenneth was gone; it wasn't right to malign the dead, and she always felt guilty, thinking of him so negatively.

Determined to move ahead, Lucy glanced at Rusty. She much preferred his open personality. With him, one always knew where one stood. Honesty and integrity formed the bedrock of his character. A woman could put her faith in a man like Rusty, she decided carefully. At this thought she realized, a little in awe, that she had taken measurable strides past her fear of a man-woman relationship. She really was healing.

They ate the blue-plate special—grilled pork chops brushed with marmalade and served with oven-browned potatoes and fresh steamed broccoli. It was surprisingly delicious, and Lucy nearly cleaned her plate.

Conversation centered on pasture conditions and Cricket's antics. Their mutual affection for the child formed a strong bridge between them, Lucy thought, smiling. And Rusty's attention never wavered from her, as if she were the only person in the diner. His eyes told her she was attractive and desirable, and a low pulsing excitement thrummed in the air.

When they finished, Lucy praised the food effusively, and an equally enthralled Beatrice pressed a jar of homemade blackberry jam into her hands—while an equally determined Rusty pushed Lucy toward the door.

"Now don't be a stranger," Beatrice admonished Lucy. "You make this ol' coyote Rusty bring you down more often."

"Mind your own business," he ordered.

"What goes on in my diner *is* my business," she shot back. Then she propped her hand on a saucily out-thrust hip. "And tonight I noticed a few sparks flyin' around my diner." She grinned at him. "You're doing real good, Rus."

"Hush, Beatrice." Rusty urged Lucy forward.

"Mmm-hmm. I always say, 'When the skillet's sizzlin', something's cooking.'" Deliberately she let her gaze fall to Rusty's proprietary hand on Lucy's spine. "Come on back real soon, y'all."

"A man might come in more often if he were to get anything to drink," Lucy heard him say loudly behind them. She realized with a smile that he never had, at that. Beatrice didn't seem to hear him. It was dark out, but the clear sky revealed thousands of diamond-bright stars. A small Asian man wearing a chef's hat and blouse and holding a saucepan stuck his head out a side door. He grinned and waved, and Lucy saluted. She assumed he was Chang, the chef.

At the truck Rusty hustled to open the passenger door and settle her inside, even stretching the seat belt safely across her hip and shoulder, and then tucking her denim coat, borrowed from Fritzy, out of the way. He treated her with charming, old-world deference, and though he'd denied this to be a date, she knew the evening for what it was.

Her plan to keep a safe distance between them didn't seem to be working, but she found she didn't mind. In fact, she hugged to herself the secret knowledge that Rusty *wanted* to date her.

"Cold?" He started the truck and put his hand on the heater knob.

"I'm not, but if you are, go ahead."

He shook his head. "Music?"

"Sure. Acid rock?"

When he jerked to face her, brows elevated, she chuckled, and amusement lit his eyes. "Scared me for a minute," he muttered. As he adjusted the radio, a soft, country ballad filled the interior. "Lucy," he said, driving leisurely, "I had a great time with you tonight.

Real great." He paused, trying harder. "Uh, I mean, it was just…nice. You're, well, you're good folks."

"'*Good folks,*'" she got out on a sputter of laughter. In the shadowed cab, she batted her eyes at him. "Rusty, are you trying to sweet-talk me?"

He darted her a rueful glance. "Not doing too well, huh? You'd think an attorney would be more articulate."

"You're doing fine." She smiled brilliantly and he stared at her as if dazed. "Um, hadn't you best watch the road?"

"What? Oh, yeah." He faced forward again, but instantly swung back. Inside, Lucy savored the possessive warmth in his eyes. She returned his gaze and felt the heat rise.

"Maybe I'd better drive," she suggested lightly.

"No." He shook his head. "That'd leave my hands free."

She got the idea. The silence grew charged, and she noticed his fingers gripped the steering wheel tighter than necessary. An aching desire heated her blood, sent a now-familiar helpless yearning through her body.

Outside her window, moonlight touched fence posts, gleamed off the lonely pavement. A tumbleweed, looking like a beachball in the dark, rolled along the roadside.

"Can I ask you something?" His voice came low-pitched and husky. "Last night, when I kissed you—"

"Let's not go there, okay?" She drew an audible breath.

"When I kissed you," he pushed on, "you seemed to like it." He sent her a hard look. "Did you?"

Watch out, Lucy, she told herself. She had no doubt

Rusty would lead her straight into bed if he could. But *he* wouldn't be the one hurting later.

"Of course I liked it," she replied carefully. "But it was just kissing, nothing more. Let's not make a mountain out of it."

"You're...comfortable with me. Right?"

"I like you," she allowed, still maintaining her bland, impersonal attitude. "You're...'good folks.'" There. That should fix him.

"Why?"

"Why what?"

"Why do you like me?" This time he kept his gaze on the road.

"Boy," she said wryly, "you didn't get to be a lawyer for nothing. I've seen starving dogs let go of juicy bones easier than you with a pet topic."

"My dad always said so," he returned. "He thought a law career would be a good fit for me. And it was. But I like being a rancher better. Now, why do you like me?"

"Okay," she said, sighing. "I give up. I like you because you're kind and—"

"*'Kind'?*" He scowled in disbelief.

"Yes." She relaxed a bit, enjoying this. "I've thought so, many times. Look how sweet you are with Cricket. You took in your brother's child with no questions asked. A lot of men would have refused such a responsibility."

"I wouldn't have turned away Tom's daughter!" Incredulity underscored his tone.

"Of course not. Not you. That's why I say you're kind. And you *are* sweet with her."

He snorted. "She's a baby."

"I've seen you work with the horses," she pointed out. "Nobody could be more patient."

"*Patient?* Are you kidding? I'm *impatient* all the time!"

"You're gruff," she corrected gently. "That's different."

"Gruff. Okay, I guess I can live with that. What else?"

Hiding a smile, she had the impression he wanted to hear masculine, powerful descriptions like hardworking, successful, even handsome or sexy. But she was having too much fun to give in yet.

"Gentle," she offered, knowing how to needle him now, but partly serious, too. "You're never rough. Even though you're a good-size man, you use your strength to work at physical labor and to protect those weaker, not to hurt."

He shifted in his seat but said nothing.

"And a woman couldn't be faulted for appreciating your broad shoulders, could she?" Lucy shrugged without apology. She guessed it wouldn't hurt to relent a bit. "And your strong legs and flat belly."

One side of his mouth kicked up. "Feel free to appreciate my belly," he offered, "or any other body parts."

"And how magnanimous you are," she returned drily. "Thank you for allowing me to admire you."

It was silent in the cab for a moment. Then Lucy considered what she found most compelling about him. "I like your eyes, Rusty." She gazed sightlessly out of the window. "I like to look at them because they're so brown and pretty—like cinnamon-sprinkled chocolate—pretty without being feminine. You're all male. A...a man's man."

Slowly she faced him and drank in his even profile.
He wanted to know what she saw in him? Well, she'd
tell him. "When I look into your eyes I see honesty.
Trustworthiness. A sturdy masculine grace. I *do* like
you Rusty, very much. The truth is, I'm wild about
you. Crazy about you. Crazy—"

Dear Lord, did I really admit that? Dismayed, Lucy
looked down at her hands and was astounded such an
admission had escaped her. She had to work to suppress a groan.

Peeping across at him, she saw all traces of amusement had fled. A strong pulse throbbed in his throat.
His jaw worked tensely. Before she could assimilate
that, he was turning off the main highway onto a little-
used dirt road. He pulled over, braking hard so the tires
slid on the dirt, and beneath a towering oak, threw the
truck into park and cut the engine.

With a flick of his thumb, his seat belt and hers came
unfastened. He reached for her, eyes hungry and dra-
matic in the darkness, and seized her into his arms.

"I can't wait anymore," he gritted out as his mouth
crashed down on hers. "Can't...wait."

The woman she'd been before might have quailed at
his intensity. But not now. A pounding wave of excitement smashed over her, like a thousand galloping
horses. Her heart lurched into thunderous beating, and
with no control whatsoever she found herself surrounding his neck with her arms, curving her body to his
hard contours. She drew in the unique scent of his skin:
healthy, like running streams and oak trees and growing things. Eagerly she kissed him back, accommo-
dated her mouth to the slant of his, aligned as much of
her frame to him as possible.

Unlike his other kisses, this was no tender caress,

but a wild onslaught, an assault strike of sexuality that demanded a reply in kind. Lucy gave it wholeheartedly.

Rusty didn't fight the hot need boiling to the surface inside him. A savage shudder ripped through his body as he surrendered to the aching desire that simmered between them all evening. From the back of his throat came a low, hoarse growl, and Lucy responded by tightening her arms about his neck with fierce determination. He hugged her closer, feeling softly rounded breasts push against his chest.

Keeping their mouths fused, he pulled her coat off her shoulders. He had to unwrap her from his neck momentarily to remove the garment, but the second she was free, she returned and sank her fingers into his hair. His hat tilted back, loose, but he didn't really feel it. Drunk on her, Rusty moved his mouth to the delicate skin of her neck, kissed every inch of her soft throat, her jaw, her ear.

With shaking, urgent fingers he began unbuttoning her blouse, hoping she wouldn't stop him, and when she didn't, his heart soared. In seconds he had the fabric open and parted and released her white bra's front catch. Her breasts spilled gloriously into his palms. Her head fell onto the seat back as he moved to take one pink nipple into his mouth.

"Rusty," she whispered breathlessly, her fingers tangled in his hair.

Her voice sounded shocked, as if she'd never before experienced such pleasure, and he thrilled to hear his name uttered thus on her lips. In the moonlight she looked like the sweetest, most fragrant peach; abruptly he realized he'd been starving for her.

"Rusty, stop." Her voice came again—urgent this

time. She was pushing at his chest. "I know you want me. And…and I want you, too. But it won't work."

"Why not?" he demanded. Rigid with need, he didn't want to stop.

"Because, because I see the end so clearly. It's coming closer—the time."

Heartbeats passed in moments of silence.

"The time for what?" But he knew. He knew.

A thin, lonely cry echoed deep inside him. How was he ever to go on without her, when their relationship was over? How would he haul out of bed each day, ride out to rope cattle, work with horses or hold his beloved Cricket—knowing that Lucy was no longer in his house, no longer waiting for him with her sunny, welcoming smile?

The cry inside wailed louder, giving him pause. He lifted his head to look, stunned, into her face, and what he saw there frightened the life out of him.

Was it love, shimmering like the purest, most valuable gold, in the depths of her eyes? Or was it a trick of the moonlight, an odd ray catching off iris and pupil—a defrauding illusion created by high sexual tension and his own demons of loneliness?

Another heavy heartbeat passed.

In the end she pushed him away, but the uncertainty reflected on his own features must have helped cool the heat between them. After a moment she lowered her gaze, withdrew to put her clothing back in order. With a wistfulness that stabbed at him, she averted her face to stare at nothing outside. He watched her chest heave in a trembly sigh, saw her fold her hands primly in her lap.

Stark regret speared through him. The moment had passed; he knew that with a sourness that filled his mouth. "Enough, huh?" he asked, already knowing the answer.

"I think so." Her voice was broken and remote.

He knew that if she didn't care, she would not sound so lost now. Strangely, her pain salved his own. Without a word he covered her shoulders with her coat, resnapped their seat belts and fired up the engine.

Weeks passed. Cricket grew like a prairie weed and now gamboled unsteadily about the house, the yard— and beneath the legs of the horses, if anyone watching took their eyes off her for two seconds. Rusty was pleased that Lucy had taken the baby to the pediatrician for checkups and immunizations, and because they didn't know her exact age, the doctor decided she was nearly one year old.

Since that evening in his pickup, never a night passed when he didn't think about it, wish for a different ending, but then conclude, bitterly, that matters were better this way. In the clear light of day, Rusty faced the painful truth: Lucy Donovan could never be his. With her impossible wealth—with her crazy dude ranch fantasy, she represented the breaking of his word to his father.

Promise me. Howard Sheffield's voice echoed in his head. *Never sell out. Keep the Lazy S in the family. Swear it.*

In the years since, his father's dream had become his own. And like the other ranchers he'd told Lucy about, he knew now that he couldn't adapt to such a change; he'd rather go broke.

The only way to keep the dream alive, keep his vow untarnished, was to buy Lucy out. There could be no compromise; she would have to go.

Even accepting this, he found that if he'd had a difficult time keeping his hands off Lucy before, now the situation became unbearable.

He wanted to stop her in the hallway, savagely back her up against the wall, feel those sweet breasts press wantonly against him. He wanted to kiss her, thrust his tongue into her mouth in a parody of what he really desired. What they both did.

At night he wanted to fall with her, both of them naked, onto his mattress, leave a light burning so he could greedily explore each rise and hollow of her skin. He wanted to skim his fingers over her shivering, gleaming flesh. He wanted her. He wanted her.

Resisting Lucy became an excruciating fight.

Stubborn and dead-set to overcome his own traitorous impulses, he reacted by stacking more work onto his already crushing load. Bulldozers and backhoes and dump trucks rumbled in to mine the gypsum, and water was diverted to his neighbor's hay fields. He cut a new deal with another company to use a gravel pit for development into, of all things, kitty litter.

The men ribbed him unmercifully about this, "Kitty litter!" Harris had howled in glee, and Rusty endured the teasing with stoicism, knowing the gravel would produce sorely needed cash.

The problem was, he was beginning to think he might not make his goal. In the beginning, he'd mapped out a schedule of monthly income he required, then made his bank deposits, and only occasionally checked the balance. Lately he'd begun opening the pass book every day, as if some fairy godmother might have flown into his office and dropped a surprise bonus into his account.

Was he fooling himself, Rusty wondered in agony? Would he make it?

Christmas arrived, bringing more joy to Lucy than she had ever found in the holidays before. During her childhood, each year her mother had casually presented her with a single gift, and always something disheart-eningly practical: at ten, Lucy had received a Tiffany lamp. "Light to do your homework by," her mother had explained. At fourteen, it was a wool wrap. Beige. "To keep you warm at boarding school." At eighteen, Lucy had been informed that she was no longer a child, and they could now dispense with the silly business of seasonal shopping and gift exchanges.

Now, on Christmas Eve, and after a delicious turkey dinner, Lucy found Fritzy hanging four red knit stockings from the mantel. Across their white-cuffed tops, names were carefully embroidered in crewel. "Rusty," one read. "Fritzy" was the next. Then, "Cricket." And to her surprise she found the last: "Lucy."

"Fritzy," Lucy exclaimed in delight. "Where did these come from?" She fingered hers with its hand-stitched scene of Santa in a sleigh bulging with toys.

"Oh, I've been working on them in the evenings," the housekeeper answered casually, waving a hand, and Lucy had a fleeting memory of red fleece being worked in the woman's gnarled fingers.

"They're lovely," Lucy breathed, pleased beyond words. "And so much fine work." On impulse, she threw her arms around the stout woman and hugged her. "Thank you. I've never had a Christmas stocking before."

Fritzy pooh-poohed her, but smiled broadly and

squeezed her back. "It's a Sheffield family tradition, didn't you know? We fill each other's stockings."

"Oh," Lucy said, thinking of the wrapped gifts she planned to place beneath the tree that evening. Earlier Rusty had dragged an eight-foot Douglas fir into the living room, set it up and then stomped out, leaving the decorating to Lucy and Fritzy. It now hung with silver stars, red bows and old baked-dough ornaments Fritzy had made years before. In dismay Lucy asked, "I'm supposed to put stuff into the other stockings?"

"Don't worry about it, dear," Fritzy assured her. "You didn't know. Next year you can."

Without replying, Lucy drifted from the room. From the top of her closet she pulled down the cardboard box she had filled with gifts, placed it on her bed and sifted through them. For Cricket she'd purchased three outfits, but the boxes were too big for her stocking. Fortunately she found a five-inch beanbag elephant that would fit. She'd already wrapped it in green-lacquered paper and tied each end with red ribbon. There was also a suitably tiny silver hair brush and comb.

For Fritzy she set aside a new apron and a silk blouse and chose a small striped perfume bottle and a bag of her favorite peppermints. These would slide nicely into the cuffed stocking tops. Lastly, for Rusty she had a yoked, red-plaid Western shirt and a bolo tie shaped like a steer's head. The bolo would fit in, and also, if she squeezed it a bit, she'd found a billed ball cap of his favorite professional football team.

She breathed a sigh of relief. Thank goodness she had things small enough; she couldn't bear it if she were the only one not to contribute to the family tradition. After all, this would hopefully become *her* tradition, as well.

Later that night when the house was quiet, she tip-toed down the shadowed stairs and placed the larger boxes beneath the tree, then moved toward the stockings with her small items.

From the fireplace red coals still glowed, casting the room in tones of tawny amber and warm vermilion. The stockings bulged with goodies, and Lucy gasped in excitement. Spiraling gold ribbons spilled from the top of hers, and it took all of her willpower not to snatch it down and rummage through. Suddenly she felt like a child in a candy store—or how she might have felt in her youth had anyone stuffed a sock and hung it, lumpy and temptingly mysterious, from the mantel. The pang she felt for what might have been lasted but a moment, and her joy remained undiminished.

Quietly she deposited her presents and moved back to her bedroom. She hummed as she brushed her teeth, drew on a nightgown and slipped into bed. It was morning before she could believe it.

"Merry Christmas," Rusty said to her from a leather chair, holding out an oversize box decorated with a huge grosgrain bow. Accepting it, she smiled, so happy she thought she might burst. A gentle rain had begun to fall sometime during the night, and it tapped against the living room windows. On the davenport where she sat with Fritzy, it was comfortable and warm.

In honor of the holiday, she wore a currant-colored sweater over a white blouse, and black slacks. From her ears dangled glittery green trees, which became Cricket's sole aspiration in life to snatch away. Laughing, Lucy fended her off and placed her on the floor with the bean bag elephant from her stocking.

Cricket played in white stretchy pants and a top decorated with dancing elves, and Fritzy had donned a long cotton holly-patterned dress. Only Rusty wore his habitual blue chambray shirt and jeans, although these were clean and carefully pressed. His black boots were shined, his hair combed.

"Thank you," Lucy said, accepting his gift. The box was heavy, and she savored its weight in her lap. "I wonder what it is. The box is so large. A new quilt for my bed," she guessed. "Or maybe a terry cloth robe?"

"You're gonna guess, are you?" Rusty teased, making as if to take the gift away. His manner had softened today, perhaps in observance of the holiday. Lucy didn't care about the reason, only that the warmth in his gaze had returned. He said, "Then you don't get it until you guess right."

"No," Lucy yelped, yanking it back. They played a friendly game of tug-of-war until Lucy won.

"For heaven's sake, open it," Fritzy urged, smiling.

Ripping off the bow, Lucy folded back white tissue and found a fawn-colored, sheepskin-lined coat—tailored in exactly her size. "It's a feminine version of yours," she exclaimed to Rusty happily, pulling it on. Thigh length, it had large front pockets and a folded-down collar. Perfect.

He shrugged, grinning. "I said you needed one of your own. And the gloves and hat I put in your stocking should match pretty well."

"It's gorgeous," Fritzy proclaimed. "It'll keep you nice and toasty." She fingered the heavy garment approvingly.

"Now open yours, Rusty." Lucy waited while he pulled the red-plaid flannel shirt from its box and then went into the other room to try it on.

"I like it. I've never had a red shirt before." Smoothing the fabric over his chest, he smiled at her.

He'd buttoned it and tucked the tails neatly into his jeans.

"Now you look Christmasy," she remarked. She wished she had the right to run her hands over his chest, too. "And I'm glad it fits you. You look good in red."

"And you look good in...brown," he said, referring to the coat she still wore, and she rolled her eyes good-naturedly. "But aren't you getting a little warm?"

"Like a roasted turkey," she replied, reluctantly letting him take it off. They laughed together, and their eyes caught and held. A moment passed. "This is my best Christmas," she told them all solemnly. "Ever. Thank you for making it so special."

Rusty shrugged, and she could tell he was a little embarrassed but also pleased by her serious tone. Fritzy clicked her tongue as if it couldn't possibly be true, but she swiped at her eyes and became very busy stacking boxes.

Fritzy ohhed and ahhed over her own gifts, presented Lucy with personalized stationery and several new hardcover bestsellers she knew Lucy enjoyed. For the remainder of the day Rusty wore the shirt and kept the ball cap on while watching football.

Cricket found the most pleasure rolling in the mountain of wadded wrapping paper and discarded ribbon. Teasing her, Rusty stuck a store-bought bow atop her head. After a moment she was distracted by a new bauble and forgot about the bow.

Lucy giggled, meeting Rusty's eyes again. "Cricket looks like a gift herself."

"She is a gift," he replied, pulling the child into his lap to tickle her.

"Yes." Privately Lucy thought that having Rusty

and the baby in her life were the most glorious gifts of all.

Late one morning, several weeks into the new year, Lucy rushed, overburdened, into the kitchen and stopped where Rusty and Harris stood drinking coffee. She nearly dropped her cargo.

Rusty rescued two grocery bags from her arms. Harris caught the other. "Where's the fire?" he asked.

"We're having a party," she announced brightly. "And we've got so much to do before tonight. Out," she commanded, dispensing a shooing wave at them. "Both of you. Out. You can't come back until five o'clock. Tell the other men they're invited."

Rusty and Harris exchanged mystified glances. "A party?" Rusty asked. "For what?"

Lucy let out an exasperated breath only a woman can properly execute. "Honestly, Rusty. It's Cricket's birthday party. She's one, remember? Now, shoo!"

At four o'clock, he stopped in against orders and found the kitchen a jumbled mess—filled with large pans of homemade lasagna, heads of lettuce ready to be washed for salad and baking flour. The flour was everywhere: it powdered the counters, streaked across Lucy's black sweatshirt and even dusted Cricket's carroty head. Wrapped gifts with bright bows tumbled across one end of the crowded counter. Flour chalked those, as well.

The playpen, empty of toys, had been shoved into a corner, and the baby crawled about the floor in a profusion of toy pots, stuffed animals and plastic building blocks. Incongruously in her chubby fist she clutched a metal potato peeler. Stepping over the piled playthings, Rusty reached down and calmly pried open her fingers to remove the sharp peeler before it could do any damage. He replaced it with a plush poodle that squeaked.

Lucy whirled. "Oh, Rusty, it's too early—what are you doing here? I'm baking a cake—Fritzy had to go to town for Cricket's gift. She left this recipe," she pointed with a floury finger at a three-by-five card, "and I've got to hurry because we need the oven for the lasagna. We've been working all day."

She stopped, only because she needed to draw air, Rusty figured. He had to suppress the urge to ask if she'd ever baked before.

"Looks like you've got things under control," he said diplomatically, and fingered a package of pointed party hats and streamers. He figured if she were this rushed at four, she'd need at least an extra thirty minutes later. Quickly he improvised. "Harris isn't sure if the men'll get the wire strung by five. Can we come at five-thirty?"

He was gratified when she shot him a relieved glance. "That'd be just right." Turning back, she began frantically cracking eggs into a bowl. The homey scene struck a satisfied chord inside him, but it was completely at odds with his fear of losing fifty percent of his heritage to her. What she wanted to do with the place froze the blood in his veins. It would chill any self-respecting rancher, he reminded himself.

Lucy was stirring lumpy batter now, biting her lip in concentration. Had it been over six months since she'd come to the Lazy S? The place had changed since her arrival. Instead of coming home to a hollow-sounding house, he found that Lucy's unique magic had transformed it into a contented family home.

She and Cricket could be any mother and daughter

in the world, getting ready for a birthday celebration. He could be the daddy.

And the husband.

Reality caught hold and knifed through him. The overwhelming workload he'd shouldered must be getting to him. He wasn't anybody's daddy, or any husband, dammit. In recent weeks he'd barely come up for air, starting long before sunup and laboring late in his office until his eyes burned.

Rusty backed out of the room and headed down the hallway. Outside the front door he paused, possessively surveying the buildings, the land, the horses and cattle.

His goal was still the same, no matter that the possibility was becoming more remote all the time. But somehow the motivation for doing so was becoming fuzzy. It seemed lately that he'd been working for something else, something completely different. Had his reasons changed?

The party was a jubilant success. Cricket sat up in her high chair, thrilled to be surrounded by so many admirers. Happily she scrubbed lasagna, cake and chocolate frosting into her hair. Everyone laughed, presented her with gifts—some homemade like the whittled steer Harris had carved—and the men sang an off-key cowboy version of "Happy Birthday."

Lucy enjoyed every minute. After these past months, she didn't think twice about changing Cricket's diaper, guarding her from danger or baking her a cake. It seemed her maternal instincts had been buried because they came bubbling up now whenever she nuzzled Cricket's soft sweet head, or felt her chubby hands clutching her neck.

"Hiyee!" Cricket cried, flinging her arms skyward. "Mamamamamama," she yelled. "Mamamamama."

"Did you hear that?" Fritzy exclaimed to Lucy. "The baby said 'Mama.'"

"Her first word," Rusty noted.

"Figured it'd be 'cow,'" Harris remarked. "Or maybe 'horsey.'"

Lucy said nothing. She wished she were Cricket's real mother. She wished she had a right to be called Mama. Getting up, she made herself very busy cleaning Cricket's fingers of chocolate frosting.

"Mamamama," Cricket shouted into Lucy's face. "Mamamamama."

Lucy froze.

"She thinks you're her mom," Harris said.

"No, it's just a sound to her. It doesn't mean anything," Lucy said quickly. So why was she so breathless? Why did her heart pound with such bittersweet longing?

"'Course she thinks you're her mom," Fritzy exclaimed. "You're the one who feeds her, takes her around, loves her. You *are* her mom, Lucy."

As if in answer, Cricket held out her arms to Lucy, demanding to be released from the high chair. "Mamamamama."

Automatically Lucy lifted the child and held her close. For some reason her gaze was drawn to Rusty's. He held a forkful of cake halfway to his mouth, but he was looking at her with a frozen expression she could not read.

Suddenly Lucy felt her chin tremble and her eyes fill. She turned, hurriedly deposited Cricket into Fritzy's arms and tried walking out of the room in casual strides, though she felt jerky and awkward.

At the hall tree she grabbed the first coat she touched—Rusty's sheepskin—because her own was in the front closet. She pulled it on and closed the front door behind her quietly. It was nearly dark, with the sun teetering on the horizon like a giant basketball about to fall through a hoop. She had no idea where she was going, she only knew she needed to think. Head down, she walked, and her wandering strides took her out into the meadow. Beneath the sheltering arms of the great oak she came to a stop.

Without thinking, she put her foot into an indentation in the trunk, hoisted herself up, climbing branch over branch, until she found the solid old limb she'd discovered as a child. The sun was lowering, spreading fading golden rays through the cobalt blue of dusk. Disconsolate and troubled, she felt more alone than ever in her life.

A movement beneath her at the trunk caught her attention and she glanced down.

Looking up at her, Rusty stood below.

Chapter Eight

Like it was a preordained act, Rusty placed his foot into the indentation at the trunk's base and scaled, hand over hand, toward Lucy. She watched him, the déjà vu of a remembered past overwhelming her. When he reached her, he settled himself near a big, whorling knot, his legs hanging down like hers, a thinner branch at his back to support him. Hatless and wearing a denim jacket, Rusty looked at home amid the rugged boughs, now mostly shorn of their spring greenery.

Through the growing gloom, he glanced at her, inscrutable, moody, saying nothing. The silence, broken only by the far-off yap of a coyote and a horse's whinny, was, if not easy, at least companionable.

He was so incredibly handsome, she thought, with his thick hair tousled, the tree's spindly limbs fanned against his back, his dark eyes speaking to her like no words ever could. Breathing deeply, she felt an odd combination of emotions: both elation and sadness. The contradictory mix made her head spin; she had to clutch a neighboring branch to keep her balance. Her fingers began to tremble, and for a moment she had to close her eyes, batter down the pain.

It touched her—Rusty's sensitivity to merely sit with her, his knowing exactly where she would be. The past rushed up to envelop her in memory of when she'd been a frightened, lonely child and he had come to her. Poignancy speared shafts of agony through her chest. Now, fifteen years later, he was still comforting her. And here they both sat again, two adults, perched like hapless owls in a tree.

Wistfully she smiled.

Rusty shifted his weight, made the sturdy branch bob. At length turned to her. "That coat," he nodded at the sheepskin, "it's mine."

It took a moment to realize he was kidding, referring back to the time he'd made the same comment to her in the barn. The time of their first kiss.

She nodded in acknowledgment, still smiling faintly. "I couldn't find mine." A second passed. "That's not true. Mine was in the hall closet, but I didn't want to take time hunting for it, so I grabbed yours."

"It looks damn good on you."

This time she chuckled, but the sound held a sad ring. "I seem to remember you saying that before. But, thanks. That's sweet."

"That's me. Kind, patient, gruff and gentle."

"A man's man," she reminded him lightly. "With an attractive belly and pretty eyes."

His familiar grin flashed. "Gotta have a good belly and eyes," he agreed, then shifted gears. "Nice party. Cricket had a ball."

Lucy stared at the stark outline of the mountains, then studied the ghostly mist gathering wraithlike over the grassland meadow. "She loved it, didn't she? I'm going to miss her, Rusty. So much." Suddenly she was afraid her voice would break, and she swallowed convulsively. "I'm going to hate leaving here."

"Leaving here?"

She grimaced, hurt by his obtuseness. "I see how hard you work. I see all the new projects you've taken on to produce revenue. It's only a matter of time, now, isn't it—when you get the money to buy me out?"

His gaze falling away, he shifted again and let out a long, rough-sounding breath.

Some unburied masochism made her prod him. "Well?" She hated this, hated sounding like a dog begging to be whipped. "Isn't it?"

"Won't make it," he muttered at the sunset.

"What?"

His quick glance revealed that all his earlier amusement had vanished like vapor rising from the grass. Clearly she could read his inner anguish, his frustrated anger. "Just before I came out here, I checked my passbook's balance." He shook his head with resentful bitterness. "Guess I've done that a million times. Anyway…I've been lying to myself. Tonight I had to face facts—we're more than halfway through the year and I've raised less than a quarter of what's needed." Twisting a small twig from a nearby branch, he stripped off the remaining leaves in short jerks.

"You're not going to make it." Careful to keep hope from her voice, she repeated his shocking statement. Every muscle in her body freezing woodenly, she couldn't be certain she'd heard him correctly.

He looked pained. "Unless I win big in Vegas, in fewer than six months, half the Lazy S will become legally yours."

Quiet delight began to well up inside her. Part of this wonderful place was really going to be hers. In her mind, future years of safety and comfort stretched ahead, filled her with visions of peace and pleasure.

Heaven on earth.

"I gave my word," he growled beside her, narrowed gaze scanning the shrouded horizon. She had a curious, fleeting impression that he saw nothing at all, that his mind was turned inward. "My vow will be broken."

"What do you mean?" She could barely hear him through the clamoring joy in her head.

"Nothing," he said.

Lucy wanted to shout out her happiness, to throw her arms around Rusty—an inclination she suppressed.

The only thing dampening her pleasure was Rusty's obvious disappointment. He didn't want her there. He didn't yet accept her. Rusty had to be satisfied, too, or everything was no good. Time was needed, she thought, lots of time for him to get more accustomed to her. Look how far their relationship had already come. Someday he would see her as a permanent part of the ranch. Everything would come to pass just as she'd planned and prayed and wished for.

Once they were lawfully bound together in business, who knew what could develop between them personally? Beyond his physical attraction, Lucy thirsted for Rusty's affection and admiration so much she was parched with the wanting. She'd get it, too, she promised herself. The future was too rife with possibility to lose heart now. Since arriving at the ranch she'd come so far. Her self-esteem had mended, her spirit had revived. Her old life of unhappiness and unfulfillment had been replaced by the rich family relationships she'd forged here.

Getting a new grip on the branch, Lucy sat up straight and felt her jaw set in newly learned determination. If she accomplished anything in her entire life, she'd make sure he ended up liking her...and accept her as part of the Lazy S.

Spirits rallying, she smiled, so incredibly thrilled she thought she might break into song. A terrible singer, she resisted the urge—instead wrapped her arms across her middle. Everything was going to be wonderful.

Later, Lucy was actually glad of her brief, completely mistaken conclusion. She came to be desperately, thoroughly, unrepentantly pleased at how very wrong her assumption had been—because later, after her heart was shattered like an old broken vase, she was able to hug the sustaining memory to her.

Yes, she thought grimly, she was *glad* she'd had that one chance to experience what it was like, if only for the briefest of her life's moments, to be truly happy.

Chapter Nine

Booming off the ranch house walls, the raised voice shattered the peaceful afternoon and put Lucy on startled notice that someone had arrived. Noisily arrived. And somebody important, she guessed. She'd gone in to collect a supposed-to-be-napping but wide-awake Cricket and bring her down. "Mamamama," the tot said, delighting Lucy down to her socks.

Now, with Cricket moored comfortably on one hip, Lucy was just descending the stairs when she heard the bellowing. She didn't recognize the gravelly masculine rumble.

"What kind of damn-fool decision is that, Rusty, to sell half the ranch?"

The shouted question brought her to an abrupt halt. *Trouble,* she thought, instantly uneasy. And last night clinging in the tree with Rusty, everything had seemed to be headed in the right direction. She could hear the low tones of Rusty's reply, but couldn't distinguish his words.

The other man thundered on. "To a *stranger?* And a woman, at that. This beats all. My God, Howard must be turnin' over in his grave."

On the last stair, dark foreboding held her still. Instinctively she clasped Cricket tight to her chest. The men were in the living room, just around the corner. In three more seconds she would have them in sight, see who was making all the racket. But she hesitated, and those three seconds dragged on as if she were rooted for three hours.

Like bats from hell, fear swooped darkly in her mind.

She inhaled a sustaining breath. Her position was solid at the Lazy S, she reminded herself, and firmly banished her doubts. No one could take away her new-found happiness.

Confidence thus bolstered, Lucy lifted her chin. Rounding the hallway corner, she took a new hold on Cricket. Soft smells of fragrant soap and the baby's own unique scent wafted from her head. Gratefully, Lucy drew it in. How she adored this child. The baby twisted forward, wide-eyed, to see the source of this loud, new voice.

The man planted in the middle of the living room stood grizzly-tall and near as big. His silver-belly cowboy hat was cocked back off his forehead, and his gnarled hands made fists on his lean hips, although age had thickened his torso. His long silver hair showed strands of its chrome color at his shirt collar. Craggy, deeply etched lines carved furrows down the sides of his face and fanned from his hard eyes. A trophy buckle, dull with age, was strapped across his middle, and his boot heels showed scuffed wear.

In his younger days, he must have been quite handsome, Lucy thought warily, noting the vestiges of good looks that still remained in his proud bearing. Yet his identity mystified her, as did his attitude. Who was he, and why was he so set against her?

At her entrance he pivoted to laser her with flat, steely eyes. "This her?" he barked at Rusty, who stood tensely nearby, gripping a half-filled coffee cup.

Rusty shot the man a disapproving glance, but gestured with his cup. "R. J. Sheffield, this is Lucy Donovan. Lucy, my uncle R.J."

"Uncle?" she repeated faintly. Animosity filled the air like a cold mist; she could feel the chill engulfing her. "I didn't know you had an uncle, Rusty." Mustering her manners, Lucy freed up one hand and held it out. "I'm pleased to meet you."

The man stared at her fingers, then squeezed them in his hamlike palm. "Wish I could say the same about you, little lady—"

"R.J.!" Rusty stepped forward, frowning.

Lucy blanched, but the big man visually raked her body as if sizing up an auction cow. "Ranch like this's a sweet plum, and you didn't waste any time hornin' in, did you? Well I don't like the bargain you've cut with my nephew, but as a businessman I've gotta give you your due." He pursed his lips, cracked with age. "It's a slick deal, one I mighta struck myself, given a similar situation."

As if in pain, Rusty's face screwed into a grimace. "Good God," he muttered. "Here we go."

Astonished at R.J.'s speech, Lucy merely blinked. He thought she was some sort of gold digger—a grasping, selfish female bent only on improving her own fortunes. In the silence R.J. stared her down. A reply

seemed warranted, but she could think of absolutely
nothing to say.

And one distressing question lit up in her mind like
a neon sign: How much influence did he have with
Rusty?

"That Tom's kid?" R.J. demanded, studying
Cricket.

Rusty exhaled and stared at the ceiling, as he always
did when struggling for patience. Lucy could almost
feel sorry for him. He replied, "Yeah, she is. Name's
Cricket."

"Cricket?" R.J. boomed. "What kinda crazy name's
that?"

"Better than Baby," Lucy mumbled, rubbing the
child's back. Cricket clung to Lucy's neck, but kept
her attention carefully on this new, noisy intruder.

"At least she's got the Sheffield red hair," R.J. allowed. "Let me see her." Before Lucy could react, he
seized the child from her arms and swung her high over
head. "There's a good baby," he crooned, "you'll be
a real good cowgirl, won't you, make your granduncle
proud?"

Lucy's gaze flew to Rusty's. He shrugged. Surprisingly, Cricket accepted this treatment without complaint, when Lucy would have expected frightened
wailing. The big man thrust the child back at Lucy.
"While the two of us talk this out," he said to Rusty,
indicating his cup, "I could use some coffee."

"I'll get it," Lucy offered. "And I think this dis-
cussion should include me."

R.J. said nothing, so she quickly moved toward the
kitchen. Once there, she sat Cricket on the floor and
handed her a soft biscuit. Fritzy was nowhere to be
seen, but there were a few dishes from lunch. When

she noticed the older woman's handbag missing from its usual spot, she remembered that Fritzy had mentioned a knitting class.

The coffeemaker was empty. Producing a fresh pot proved a chore: she fumbled the measuring scoop, sprayed grounds across the counter, spilled water pouring it into the reservoir. The task accomplished at last, she fidgeted nervously as the brew dripped and she strained to hear the men's conversation. Obviously R.J. didn't like her, and disliked what she had done. Well, she found him rude and pushy in turn. She hoped Rusty wouldn't give his opinion any weight. She wished he would just go away.

Like poison arrows, voices speared in from the living room.

"Why didn't you come to me for the money?" she heard R.J. demand.

"I haven't seen you for years," Rusty replied. She heard the clank of his mug banged forcefully onto the sideboard. "What makes you think I'd run to you, begging for money?"

So much for waiting for her to start the conference.

"Well, dammit, boy, we're family. That rift I had with your daddy was years ago, back when I moved to Dallas and started my own spread. But that don't mean I wouldn't help if you were in trouble. 'Specially now that Tom and Landon are gone."

Lucy waited for Rusty to explain that Tom and Landon were solely responsible for the ranch's financial straits and not Rusty himself. But when he kept silent, she was proud he didn't assign blame. At every turn he had accepted life's obligations. He didn't run from problems but faced them head-on.

Coffee finished, Lucy grabbed the steaming carafe

and a clean mug and encouraged Cricket to follow. She had to get in there and protect her interests, she thought urgently. Rushing into the living room, she found R.J. perusing an old wall-hung photograph of Howard, lounging on a corral rail, flanked by his three boys and proudly grinning into the camera.

Cricket toddled in, gnawed her biscuit and promptly found her beanbag elephant to play with. She stuck the soft trunk into her ear.

"Here's coffee." Lucy struggled for a dignified air. She had to concentrate to pour steadily. R.J. made off-hand thanks, and she moved with the decanter to where Rusty held his ground beside the davenport. Belatedly she noticed he was wearing the red-plaid shirt she had given him for Christmas. It made no sense to do so, but she took heart from that. She lifted his cup from the sideboard, filled it and held it out like an offering.

Needing reassurance, she searched his eyes. Her own were pleading, she knew, but she was helpless to mask her concern. A simple warm smile from Rusty, an encouraging nod, any sign at all would do wonders for her nerves.

No smile or nod came forth. Except for his earlier grimace, he held an enigmatic, reserved mien, giving her little. Was there a touch of coolness where she usually found warmth?

Her foreboding bloomed, flowered into full anxiety. Coolly, Rusty inspected his coffee, then his thumbnail. Still nothing.

Suddenly she couldn't face his detachment and hunched a shoulder away. Her eyes squeezed shut. *No,* she cried inside, *don't let anything happen to change things.*

Abruptly R.J. lumbered to an overstuffed easy chair

and eased his bulk onto the cushions. "Ah, that's better." He sighed. "These old bones creak something awful nowadays. Had my pilot fly me into Reno this morning—and sittin' in that cramped seat didn't do me any good. Now I'm glad I had the idea of stoppin' in here." Taking a draught of his coffee, he leveled a thoughtful glance at his nephew. "Sit down, son."

Rusty shook his head and Lucy stood grasping the half-filled carafe, feeling awkward and ignored. Frightened. She felt the slightest bit dizzy, as if she were adrift on a rocking boat.

"Suit yourself." R.J. crossed a knee with one booted foot. "Rusty, from what you tell me, according to the terms of your agreement with the woman—" Lucy recognized that meant her "—it's not too late to set matters right. I won't allow the ranch my granddaddy founded to be split up. I'll wire you the money straight away."

Lucy froze, a storm of chilled dread icing her insides like an Arctic winter. Unblinking, she stared at Rusty, but still she could not read his thoughts.

"I'll advance you the balance due," R.J. finished matter-of-factly, "and the Lazy S can return to its rightful *family* hands." He focused on Lucy. "Sorry, Miz Donovan. You had a good run at it. But business is business. You understand."

Blindly Lucy took a stumbling step back and bumped against an oak tea cart. Groping behind her, she curled frozen fingers around the edge with one hand, somehow still hanging on to the carafe with the other. A tiny wave of coffee slurped out onto the carpet. She stared numbly at the spreading stain.

"R.J.," Rusty commanded quickly, "I think we'd

better hash this out in my office.'' He began to walk toward the room in back.

And not in front of Lucy, she inferred. Inside, she felt her world sinking—her rocking boat now a doomed, badly listing ship. With disaster looming at the bottom of the sea, she found it difficult to breathe.

On the easy chair, her worst nightmare turned his attention to Cricket. ''The child'll come and live with me, Rus. You got no proper home for her here, and my daughter and her husband'll open their arms to her.''

Across the room, Rusty stiffened. ''You mean Julie...and Dan? Why would they want Cricket?''

R.J. shrugged. ''Been married six years, tryin' for a baby all that time and no luck. I know for a fact Julie and Dan would jump at the chance to take Cricket here. She's a pretty thing, and seems to have a good enough temperament. Gotta change her name, though.'' He rubbed his jaw. ''Katherine, maybe. Or Margaret.''

Katherine! Lucy thought. Margaret! Her baby's name was Cricket, she wanted to scream. Cricket.

She stopped breathing altogether, her chest crushed as if by an anvil. She was drowning in a frigid sea of disbelief. *You're going to lose the ranch,* she told herself in shock. *And precious Cricket, too. Most of all, you're going to lose Rusty.*

Something vivid and alive inside her shriveled.

Of all the possible developments she'd considered, none included a wealthy relative turning up to finance Rusty, and to take the child, too. It was impossible. Unbelievable.

Dropping both feet to the floor, R.J. leaned toward the child and held out a beefy, sun-spotted hand. ''Come here, kid. You'll come home to Dallas, and in a year or so old Grandpa R.J.'ll buy you a pony.''

Willing Cricket to shrink away from this invader, Lucy wanted the baby to show him he wasn't wanted, that she would go exactly nowhere with him. *Cricket loves me,* Lucy thought desperately. *I'm Cricket's caretaker, her nurturer, her constant port of maternal love.*

Lucy was Cricket's mother, if only in her heart.

But the tiny girl spied a glittering flash on the man's hand and reached out to touch his gold ring. As always, Cricket's lively curiosity ruled her, Lucy thought, chin trembling. It wasn't the baby's fault—she was a child, inquisitive and impulsive—she couldn't know about an adult's unrealistic hopes and fears. Cricket's enthusiasm for life was one of the things Lucy loved about her.

Clearing her throat, Lucy struggled to find her voice. When she did, it sounded like a rusted gate, creaking in the wind. "Rusty, you wouldn't—you won't go along with this—with R.J.'s...plan, will you?"

R.J. cut in. "'Course he will. You've lost, girl. Start packing."

"R.J.," Rusty said through gritted teeth. "Dammit, that's rude, even for you. We'll talk in my office. *Now.* He faced her. "Lucy, I need some privacy with my uncle. You and I will discuss things later tonight, okay?"

The older man unfolded stiffly from the chair.

Everything she had ever hoped for seemed to come whirling crazily down to this one moment. Frantic, she searched Rusty's face. It was slipping away, her dream an empty raft rushing over endless falls. Now that she was so close to losing everything, how easy it was to admit that she was in love with him. On some level, hadn't she known this immutable fact? Hadn't she *always* known? From the depths of her woman's heart, she was brim-full with emotion. All the longing in her being found its nucleus in this one man.

To her he symbolized safety in a dangerous world. Even when he wasn't aware of it, he was kindness. He was bold and strapping and healthy—her investment in the future. He was love.

Like a powerful tide, the truth washed over her. She wanted to live with the man, to wake up beside him, to kiss him every morning and evening and sometimes in between. She wanted, oh Lord, she wanted to be his wife.

But she had no real evidence that he held such deep need for her. Physical desire, yes, indeed. And he enjoyed the camaraderie between them. Perhaps he even felt a certain appreciation for her. But love?

The time of reckoning had come.

"*Rusty,* please," Lucy whispered hoarsely. "You're not going to do this. You won't accept your uncle's money." She made each statement knowing in her heart it would be sheer idiocy if Rusty *didn't* take R.J.'s offer. Why give up something so important if he didn't have to?

Only love could provide the answer.

"Yes," he replied, reducing her already gossamer-light confidence to a windblown dandelion. "I might take him up. I'm going to weigh his terms, and then later you and I will work things out between us." He sent her a speaking glance. "Understand? We'll talk later."

Without awaiting her answer, the two men moved to the office and closed the door after them. To Lucy, the muted click held all the finality of a slammed steel gate.

The men remained closeted in the office while Lucy paced the house, but she had no direction, no idea why she had to keep moving, only that dread kept her in jittery motion. Realizing all the walking was silly, she climbed the stairs to the bedroom, taking Cricket and a warm formula bottle. At her quilted bed she sank down to feed the baby.

As usual, Cricket wanted to hold the bottle, so Lucy had nothing to do but cradle her. She allowed her gaze to wander and for the first time took stock of her belongings: suits, slacks, jeans and blouses in the closet. Three perfume bottles and makeup in a basket on her white wicker chest of drawers. A few novels. An impressive stock portfolio she'd long ignored. Her sports car. Cash in the bank.

She'd thought she would soon own part of this ranch.

Stuff. Inwardly she scoffed at herself. Things, that's what belonged to her. All material objects, and even valuable in the view of the outside world. But the intangible substance in life she'd always yearned for still eluded her. That's why she'd come here, to find a home, to find people who needed her as much as she needed them. To find the man from her youth whom she'd never forgotten.

She wished Rusty were in love with her.

A short burst of ironic laughter bubbled from her throat, instantly swallowed by a sob. Not likely. From the start he'd made her understand—even in their warmest moments—that the Lazy S was of primary importance to him. He would do anything to keep it.

Miserable, she felt her eyes mist over. Nothing of what she'd tried so hard to achieve had come to fruition. In her arms, Cricket worked on the bottle. If she'd given birth to this child herself, she couldn't love her more.

But when she thought of the settled home R.J.'s daughter could provide for the baby, she felt inadequate and inferior. Cricket deserved a normal family upbringing, with a properly married father and mother. R.J.'s daughter could provide what Lucy could not.

Rusty was obviously getting ready to oust her. A stabbing knife, the stark conclusion ripped through her. Naturally he would accept his uncle's help, of course he would. Wasn't it what he'd worked and slaved for during these short months—to buy her out? And hadn't he been terribly disappointed last night when he'd been forced to admit his efforts were on a collision course with failure?

R.J.'s fortuitous arrival must seem a godsend.

Now there would be no further need or use for her. Lucy Donovan had just become superfluous—worse—unwanted on the Lazy S Ranch.

"I'll tell him I'm leaving," she said aloud. Even to her, her voice sounded raw and unconvinced. Leave, she repeated silently. To leave here.

Knees shaky, she forced herself to enter the adjoining bathroom, rinse her face and school her features into a polite mask. In the mirror her cheeks and jaw appeared slightly puffy, and her eyes looked like brittle green glass. Taking another moment, she brushed her hair and tried harder to compose herself.

At last there was nothing else to do. Collecting Cricket, she went downstairs and started for Rusty's office.

The closed door loomed like a forbidden portal, and behind it she could hear the sounds of low conversation. Her strides slowed. Inside was one man who disliked her and another who'd shortly be carting out her suitcase—just as he'd carted it in months ago.

Courage fled.

All at once she knew she couldn't brave them, not the two who even now were plotting her removal.

With a heavy gait she retreated to her bedroom. It didn't take long, actually, to pack her belongings and drag them downstairs. Given the circumstances, what other option did she have? Her large suitcase made thumps on the steps as she pulled it along, and she had a brief, secret hope that Rusty would materialize from his office, demand to know what she thought she was doing. "Take everything back upstairs," he insisted in her vision. "You belong here. I'll never allow you to leave me. You hear, Lucy Donovan? Never."

The fantasy faded, and the office door remained as obstinately closed as if mortared shut by sturdy bricks.

Because Cricket was beginning to fuss, Lucy left her things in the entry and went to buckle the baby into the kitchen high chair for a late snack. This might be the last meal she ever fed Cricket, she realized in despair, slicing fresh pear chunks onto the tray.

Out in the entry hall, the screen door slammed and Fritzy blew in like a gray whirlwind, accompanied by Harris. "Where's Rus?" Fritzy asked. Both turned questioning glances her way.

Afraid to trust her voice, Lucy became extremely busy feeding Cricket until the silence drew out and she was forced to offer a reply. She spoke around the knot in her throat. "Um," she managed in fragmented sentences, "in his office. With his uncle. With R.J." At the end she had to swallow a watery gulp, but she thought she sounded okay.

His eyebrows raised, Harris whistled through his

mustache. "R.J.'s visiting? He hasn't shown up here for years. Wonder what he wants?"

"The ranch," Lucy croaked before she could stop herself. With considerable effort she sucked in a shallow breath and concentrated very hard on wiping pears from Cricket's cheeks.

From the corner of her eye, she thought she saw Harris and Fritzy exchange perplexed glances.

"Well, that's R.J.," Fritzy said, moving her box aside, "he's a hard man to figure."

I found his intentions pretty damn clear, Lucy wanted to scream.

"If R.J.'s come all this way, it must be important. The truck can wait until later." Harris shrugged and touched his hat. "Have a good day, now." He was gone.

Drained, her nerves frayed like an old rope, Lucy began to wonder if she might completely unravel. She shot to her feet. "Fritzy, I'm leaving. Can you take Cricket? I've bathed and fed her."

"Of course I'll take the little lamb. Let's just put her in the playpen while I clean up here." With efficient movements the woman tied an apron about her girth and began to soap the lunch dishes.

"To the playpen with you," Lucy sang out, attempting a light tone. She swung the baby inside. Leaning down, she tenderly pressed her lips to the baby's fragrant head and laid a hand along the plump folds of her neck. "I love you," she whispered, agonized. "I love you."

For one mad, crazy moment she considered snatching the child up and running away with her. It would be so easy really, to buckle her in a car seat and drive away.

It wouldn't be right, though. Lucy knew that Cricket was going to a good home. It was best for Cricket, Lucy admitted to herself, if she simply walked out of the child's life. She had to do it now, with no further contact. Why prolong matters?

Her heart clenched. This was brutal, this goodbye. She would rather cut off her arm than wrench away. Her throat ached and her legs felt wobbly.

Trembling, she bit her lip, then before she could break down completely, she rushed up to Fritzy's back and hugged her from behind. "Oh, Fritzy, thank you. Thank you for everything." On the last word her voice broke and she turned to stumble out.

"What in the world..." Bewildered, Fritzy craned over her shoulder, fingers dripping soapy water onto the floor.

Lucy could barely see for the cloudy film blinding her, but she managed to snatch up her suitcase and purse and fumble for the keys. Shoving the case into the car's trunk, she threw herself into the driver's seat and twisted the key. At this time of year the afternoons were short. Already the sun dipped low on the horizon, casting the barn in long shadows. It was coat weather, but she didn't stop.

Rusty would be surprised, probably, at her precipitous departure; he might even miss her briefly, but ultimately he'd be relieved. No awkward farewell scenes to deal with, no empty, false promises to keep in touch. No bother. Lucy had little doubt this way was best.

Chapter Ten

Where to go? What to do?

Lucy's dilemma finally struck her after she'd driven a good ten miles down Interstate 80. It was fully dark now, with the light of a three-quarter moon the only illumination besides her headlights. Lost in a hazy fog of misery, her brain felt sluggish, her body listless. She had long since sold the home she and her husband had owned, and she'd no relatives left. After Kenneth died, she lost all contact with the few people she had called friends. No one was expecting her. No one waited for her, worried about her. There wasn't a single person to keep a light burning.

A lost soul, that's what she was.

As she faced the truth, a broken sigh issued from her: Lucy Donovan was twenty-six years old and had no home. With nothing else to do, she simply kept driving.

Wealthy and homeless, she thought with sad irony. A pitiful twist, but it proved one thing: money alone didn't make a person happy. If only a miracle occurred and Rusty would love her, she'd gladly give away every dime.

She could not stop thinking about him. Before R.J. came storming into her life and stripped her of everything she held dear, the only problems between her and Rusty involved her dude ranch plans—aside from his fully accepting her imminent partnership. However, she considered that a minor contention. Over time it would have been naturally resolved.

Rolling down the window, she let her hair blow wildly about her head in the cool evening wind. The temperature hovered around fifty degrees, cold enough for a coat, except Lucy had none. With a pang she recalled Rusty's beautiful sheepskin gift and how she hadn't wanted to take time to fetch it. Now she regretted her carelessness. The coat was something he'd given her, something, however inanimate, to remember him by.

Shivering, she thought of Rusty's coat, wished she were snuggled inside the furry warmth, enveloped by his scent. The chill wind raised gooseflesh on her arms, but she welcomed the discomfort. Maybe it would lift a measure of the murky fog oppressing her.

Were her notions and Rusty's so at odds she had completely alienated him? If her heart could sink any further into abysmal melancholy, it did so now. She'd ruined everything, she decided, by pushing her own selfish aspirations onto him.

The wide open land rolled past. Rock groupings, sagebrush and a few stunted yucca made dark humped shapes in the wild country, and across the road before her, a taupe-winged owl skimmed low. Few vehicles passed by, and the air was pristine. Nevada was stark and lovely, she thought. It would be a shame if crowds of littering, smog-producing people came to ruin its peaceful harmony.

For the first time she considered Rusty's perspective.

He didn't want noisy mobs trampling his land. Of course he wanted to keep private what he'd fought so hard to safeguard. She sighed. Now that it was too late, matters were swiftly becoming more absolute.

Regret ate at her. If only she could go back and change things. With all her enthusiastic talk of sharing the bucolic countryside, she'd put a wedge between them. If she were honest, she'd admit that R.J. wasn't the problem. He had just provided the hammer that drove the wedge home.

Miles slipped by until up ahead she noticed a break in the highway, an old shantylike gasoline station and another larger structure with a sign that read Beatrice's Diner. She hadn't even thought about stopping, but now her empty stomach reminded her she'd eaten nothing since lunch, and she pulled in next to several pickups and rusted sedans, noting the place appeared about half-full. That was fine—she'd be served quickly and on her way in no time. The idea of hanging around a moment longer than necessary was distasteful. She did want to say goodbye to Beatrice, though. At their one meeting, Lucy had liked her.

Taking her purse, she locked the car and paused in the doorway of the diner. Behind her, out on the highway, a white sheriff's patrol car winged past, lights flashing. Lucy wondered what could motivate the police into such a hurry. An accident? A fire? Burglary? She shrugged.

Inside, the usual assortment of families, stove-up old cowhands and young waddies lounged at the counter and occupied several tables. Just inside she hesitated so her eyes could adjust to the slightly darker interior.

"Lucy, my stars! Don't stand in the doorway, honey, come on in."

Still unaccustomed to the dim light, Lucy peered over the counter. Behind it stood Beatrice herself, waving her forward. The woman wore her habitual white apron, and impossibly, her beehive hairdo was teased higher than before, her lipstick painted an even more brilliant crimson. She grinned, showing her characteristic protruding teeth.

With an effort, Lucy mustered a smile as she moved in dragging steps, the best she could do. "How are you, Beatrice?"

"Happy as a flea in a doghouse," Beatrice sang out cheerfully. "And how're you—you're lookin'..." She paused, faltering, as she took in Lucy's wind-mussed hair, slumped shoulders and shadowed eyes. "Uh, mighty fine."

Apathy weighing her down, Lucy found she barely cared how she looked. She started to slide onto a stool at the counter; then, wanting to avoid idle conversation with anyone, she changed her mind and pointed to a small, nearby booth. "This okay?"

"Sure, honey." Beatrice frowned, hurrying around the counter with her coffee pot and a mug. She placed the filled mug before Lucy. "Is everything all right?"

Lucy let her gaze drift around the diner. "I suppose. I'm just...I thought I'd get something to eat. I didn't have much lunch today."

The woman studied Lucy's face a long moment, still frowning. "All right. I'll just grab a menu."

Lucy nodded. She stared at the steam rising in serpentine coils from the coffee but didn't touch it. After she ate, she'd have to leave. Get in her car. Drive away.

For no reason at all her hunger suddenly fled.

Beatrice's arched brows were pinched as she returned with a menu, sugar and a little pitcher. "Here's real cream, just how you like it." She bent forward to search Lucy's face again. "Well, go on," she urged after a moment passed and Lucy made no move.

Lifting her hands from her lap, Lucy nodded and obediently stirred in the cream. It was nice, having someone care if she looked like a rodent the cat dragged in or whether she drank her coffee cold or hot. "You're so thoughtful, Beatrice." Belatedly, she remembered her manners. "Thank you for the cream."

The proprietor straightened and crossed her arms. "How's things up at the Lazy S? That Rusty been treatin' you all right?"

"What?" Startled, Lucy glanced up. "Oh, yes. He's—he's treated me fine." That much was true. He hadn't done anything immoral or illegal or even rude. How could she explain that her hopes had simply been unrealistic? How could she tell this well-meaning woman that her heart had splintered into a thousand scattered pieces?

Hunched over the coffee, Lucy made a production of tasting it. She opened her menu and ordered the first thing her eye fell upon, chicken salad. Avoiding Beatrice's all-seeing gaze, she studied a sore cuticle on her index finger.

Staring at her a moment longer, Beatrice licked a stubbed pencil and scratched the order on a pad she dug from her apron pocket. She appeared about to make one of her pithy comments, then thought the better of it. A low warble sounded from somewhere behind the counter, and Lucy dully realized it was a ringing telephone.

"I'll just get that," Beatrice said. Whisking away, she took up the receiver, listened, then darted a glance at Lucy. Although completely uninterested, Lucy couldn't help hearing snatches of the conversation. Bea seemed to be arguing with someone.

"If women are foolish, it's only because the good Lord made them a match for men," Bea declared crisply to the person on the other end. With that she turned her back, muttered a few more annoyed comments, then finished with the barely audible, "I'll try. What? I said I'll do what I can. This is obviously your own damn fault." With a flourish, she hung up.

Lucy's simple order seemed to take longer than necessary, and when it did come, she picked at the food. She knew Beatrice's meals were delicious, but right then the salad seemed utterly tasteless. At last she laid her fork down.

Catching Beatrice's attention proved easy, as the woman kept shooting her concerned glances. "May I have my ticket, please?" Lucy asked.

Nodding, Beatrice drew her pad from her pocket and tore off a sheet. Before she placed it on the table, she took a long inventory of the brightly lit parking lot out the front window. "Here you go." Distracted, she started to move back to her post behind the counter, but Lucy already had her money out. "I'll just get your change," Beatrice said, glancing again out the window.

Vaguely wondering what could be of interest, Lucy craned her neck but saw only parked vehicles. She shrugged.

At the cash register, Beatrice fumbled in the drawer, then slammed it shut. "Lucy," she said, "for some

reason I don't have the right change. You'll stay a minute while I get some from the safe in back, won't
you?"

"Sure." Lucy collected her purse and set it in her
lap.

"Fine. I'll just be two shakes. Now, you won't
leave?"

"No, I'll be here." It wasn't like she was needed
anywhere. Tiredly she rubbed her temples.

Long minutes passed while Lucy waited for Beatrice
to return. When she didn't come back, Lucy hesitantly
got to her feet beside the booth. Hopefully there were
no kitchen emergencies for Bea to deal with. Should
she go looking?

Just then Bea emerged from the swinging doors.

"Here you are." She placed several dollar bills and
change into Lucy's hand. Glancing over Lucy's shoulder, she again perused the parking lot. "Sorry it took
so long. My chef, Chang, had a devil of a time getting
the safe open. Seems we forgot the combination!" She
laughed lightly.

"So you finally remembered it?" Lucy dropped the
change in her purse and tucked the dollar bills under
her lunch plate.

"Huh? Oh! Yeah, that's it. We remembered it. Silly
us." Beatrice beamed.

"That's good."

At her back a small man with Asian features and
wearing chef's attire poked his head out the swinging
doors. As Bea swung around, he nodded at her, quickly
bowed and withdrew. Chang, Lucy recalled—Beatrice's cooking, safe-cracking chef.

Lucy breathed in deeply and faced the other woman.

"You've been awfully nice to me. So I should tell you I won't be around any more. I'm—"

"Wait! I completely forgot." Bea slapped her forehead. "My sister's grandkids—you've got to see their pictures. They just came in the mail—really adorable. Hold on." Before Lucy could protest, Beatrice rummaged in a cabinet beneath the register.

"Here." Folded in a plastic waffle case, the photos numbered at least forty, and they were displayed on both sides, Lucy saw. When Bea shook the case, it fell open like an accordion. The collection had to be closer to eighty, Lucy thought in dismay.

Shoving aside Lucy's mug and plate, Beatrice scooted into the booth and pointed opposite. "Go on. Sit."

Politely, Lucy sank onto the edge of the vinyl seat and tried to appear interested, while the other woman regaled her with exploits of her sister's grandchildren. The showing took a good ten minutes before Lucy could courteously excuse herself. She liked Beatrice and appreciated her kind heart, but inside, Lucy ached miserably.

Regretfully refusing more entreaties to study the photographs again, she actually had to back out of the diner.

Beatrice followed.

"Really, you don't have to walk me to my car," Lucy protested. "Don't neglect your customers on my behalf."

"It's no trouble." Like a nervous hen, Bea scurried after her. "They'll wait for me."

Outside now, in the pool of overhead lamps, Lucy hesitated, key at her car's door. The wind gusted, tugged at her blouse and made Beatrice's apron flap on her legs. "Bea, are you feeling all right? You're acting a little…uh, strange."

Bea squinted down the dark highway, her hands twisting. "Just need a little fresh air, but my, it is getting windy, isn't it? Now, where're you headed, honey? Back to the ranch?" She asked this last on a hopeful note.

"Er, not exactly." Lucy slipped inside and tossed her purse onto the passenger seat. She closed her door but rolled the window down. "I tried telling you before. Things…didn't work out for Rusty and me. I…I have to leave."

"Oh, Lucy." Beatrice gazed at her sadly. "I don't know the problems, but everything can be worked out, can't it?"

The lump that had formed in Lucy's throat that morning began to grow again. She started her engine and shook her head. "There's nothing I want more, but…I don't think so." She looked at the woman, who, under other circumstances, might have become her friend. "Thanks, Beatrice. Goodbye."

Backing the car up, she shifted into drive and started rolling. The asphalt street by the diner was old, with uneven potholes and loose gravel making driving bumpy. Preoccupied and gloomy, she didn't notice anything unusual for thirty or forty yards.

When the road smoothed out, her car still bumped on the right side, so she braked and pulled over. *What now?* While no longer in the full glare of the diner's parking lot lamps, she figured there was still enough light to see any problem. Getting out, she walked around to examine the tire and found a long slash in the rubber tread.

She never knew what made her swing around at that

particular moment to glance at the diner. Yet she spotted a dark head in a chef's hat peeking out the back door. Chang was observing her, but why? In his hand something glinted in the moonlight, and she made out the shape of a curved paring knife. When he saw Lucy notice him, he quickly ducked back inside.

At the front of the diner, Beatrice was still poised outside the glass doors. Lucy thought she saw Bea heave a long-relieved sigh.

What was going on?

Just then, an old pickup truck roared up in a squeal of tires and flurry of sprayed gravel. In the rising wind, dust billowed, making Lucy cough. The truck ground to a halt next to her car. Half-blinded by the headlight's glare Lucy shaded her eyes and took in the unique shape of the driver's profile.

Rusty.

She caught her breath, and her heart soared and then just as quickly plummeted. Whatever he wanted to say couldn't be good. Probably he was just mad she hadn't said goodbye.

Jerking open his door, he slid out and slammed it shut, a black scowl darkening his handsome features. He wore the same jeans and red-plaid shirt she'd last seen him in, but had jammed on his black felt cowboy hat and wore it pulled low over his forehead. With the light at his back, she couldn't make out his eyes.

"Lucy, where the hell do you think you're going?" he demanded thunderously. He planted both hands on his hips. "With Highway 80 the only road around, I took a chance and called the sheriff to the north to be on the lookout for you. Then I phoned Beatrice here, figuring somebody had to have seen you. It's lucky she had you here, or I'd have to go driving over half of Nevada. Well?''

Lucy lowered her gaze to the ground. She found it difficult to look at the man she loved so much, knowing he didn't love her. ''My car's got a flat,'' she told him unnecessarily.

''Thank God for that,'' he said.

From the corner of her eye, she saw him twist around and nod meaningfully to Beatrice. Bea smiled, then turned with a satisfied air to disappear inside the diner.

Rusty swung around to face Lucy. ''Right when R.J. was taking off, Fritzy rushed up, all aflutter, said you'd hightailed it out. She was real upset. I checked your room, Lucy. You cleaned it out, didn't you? So I'm asking you,'' he demanded again, ''*where are you going?*''

With a shift in his weight, muted lamplight reached his eyes. Even knowing he was angry, she was shocked to see that his eyes blazed savagely, like hard amber gems. His shoulders were high and tensed, his color flushed. His hands were shaking. How well she knew that a man on the edge of rage was unpredictable, dangerous. Kenneth had blown up at her frequently, shouted her down, frightened her. He'd used his anger as a weapon to cow her, force his will upon her.

Yet somehow Rusty's fury didn't alarm her. As enraged as he appeared, she was not afraid. Although she had lost the most precious things in life a person can lose, her time spent on the Lazy S had taught her to believe in herself. She realized that even if matters didn't work out this time, she did have a great deal to offer a husband, to children, to the world.

Lifting her gaze, she stared into Rusty's flashing

eyes and knew she had mended emotionally and spiritually.

Putting her hands on her own hips was unlike the old Lucy—the meek, uncertain woman she'd been just six months before. It felt alien and aggressive. And, damn it, good.

"All right," she began, raising her chin, "I'll tell you. I'm going to Reno. Or Vegas. I don't know. Maybe I'll just keep driving right on through to California, buy a bikini, spend some time on the beach, not that it's any of your business. Why, Rusty? Why do you want to know?"

Like a bull about to charge, he thrust his face down to her level. "You can't just leave," he told her forcefully. "Who'll patch up the men when they get hurt? Who'll paint the house and mow the lawn?"

Despite her self-confidence, Lucy felt her lips tremble. She'd loved performing those tasks. Then the ludicrousness struck her and she almost laughed. "A nurse?" she suggested. "A handyman?"

"You don't say a word to anybody, don't mention that you're moving out. What am I supposed to do?"

As quickly as it had come, her amusement fled, rapidly replaced by her own anger. Who the hell did he think he was—highhandedly chasing her down to shout at her about mowing lawns and such?

Going up on tiptoe so they were nose to nose, she scowled as fiercely as he did, and gave him as good as she got. "Enjoy full ownership of your ranch, I guess. I can't imagine why you're complaining. For months you've done nothing but work to try and get rid of me. Well, you got your wish." On this last her voice rose, matching his in decibels.

Deep inside, she felt a welling of healthy catharsis,

a washing clean of her wounds. She could return Rusty's anger and hold her own in an argument with him without fear of reprisal. Boy, she thought in fleeting wonder, it sure felt right. The only thing missing was an intact heart; the pieces had scattered to the four winds. She loved him.

"Who's going to take care of Cricket—love her like a real mother—like you do?" Ruthlessly he used the baby to bruise her.

That hurt, but she couldn't let him see. Mostly shredded into ribbons, her pride was a beaten thing, but vestiges somewhere deep inside still remained.

"I don't care," she lied.

Moving faster than she could react, he grabbed her by the shoulders and gave her a shake. "You care," he gritted out.

Her eyes went wide, yet still she was unafraid. No haunting memories came back to remind her of past terror, no panicked emotions arose to swamp her. Truly, she was healed. With every fiber in her being she knew that Rusty would never hurt her.

"You care," Rusty repeated, harsh and low, "because you love Cricket. And you love…me. Say it, Lucy. Say you love me, or all my work is for nothing. I'm for nothing."

She stared at him. "I…don't understand. What do you mean? You've worked like the devil to get rid of me—"

He shook his head. "To keep you. I want you on the Lazy S."

Completely bewildered, Lucy reached up to rest her palms on his chest. He was so close—still grasping her shoulders—she could not resist touching him. He was so solidly muscled, his flesh vibrant and powerful beneath her fingers. And he smelled familiar...and wonderful. Like wild sage and saddle leather. She shook her head to focus.

"Rusty, what about your uncle? What about R.J.?"

"I sent him away," he said impatiently. "We had a long talk, worked out a lot of old problems. But I didn't accept his loan. For a while I thought it might be the answer, borrowing money from him to pay you back right away. But he hasn't really changed. I saw there would be too many strings attached." He grimaced. "R.J. likes to control things."

Lucy held her breath. "And Cricket?"

"Cricket's my baby," he stated. "And yours. We're her family—you and me, and Fritzy. We can do the best by her—not some cousin in Dallas. Lucy, how could you think I'd let anyone take her off?"

Lucy's eyes began to fill, and something she'd thought dead inside came to life. "I don't know," she whispered, feeling more open and vulnerable than ever before. "I don't know."

He wasn't gripping her anymore, but making tiny, kneading motions with his hands on her arms. It was cold outside, she thought fleetingly. Very cold. Wind whipped her hair around her face, stung her neck. The only place on her body that felt warm was where he touched her. Did he realize he was caressing her?

Rusty continued, "R.J. left, but I made him an invitation to come back and visit."

Could she be hearing him correctly? Some demon forced her to blurt, "If you'd accepted his offer, you'd be shut of me now."

"Why would I want to lose a beautiful woman who loves me? I'm asking you again—now—to say it,

Lucy. God help me, but I'm going crazy. I need to know I'm right about this. Tell me.''

She wanted to; the words trembled on her mouth. It would be such a relief to express how she felt, how she'd always felt. Even if she started now and kept telling him until the end of her life, he'd never know the depth of her love.

But she couldn't go back to how things were before, with the sword of his debt to her hanging over her head. She heaved in a breath so deep it hurt.

"Rusty, when you do make enough to repay me…will I have to leave the ranch?" Aching, she stared up, afraid to blink, afraid of his answer.

Abruptly he let her go, pivoted aside and studied the ground. With his chin angled away, his hat shielded his face from her. She could only see his carved jaw.

Without his touch, her arms went as cold as the rest of her, and her teeth started to chatter. How frigid the world became when one was alone, she thought in passing, and how warm it could be when one had somebody to love.

He loomed before her, his body an enigmatic shadow. She could feel tension vibrating off him in waves. "When you first came to me," he said, "I admit, I slaved night and day to keep the ranch in my hands. But over time, after I got to know you, my motivations changed." He paused and stole a glance at her.

"Changed?" she prompted. She had an incredible notion that his next statement would be of great import. Whatever he said now could alter the entire course of her life.

"You don't get it, do you?" He blew out a tense breath. "Of course not. I realize I'm not making much sense, but finding you'd packed up and moved out really threw me. Somehow I got the idea I'd never see you again. Something in me just...panicked. I had to find you. I had to."

A strong gust of wind threatened to unseat his hat, so he took a moment to screw it down tight. He appeared to be gathering himself, and finally he faced her square on.

"I...*have* to repay you, no matter what. That's what all my work became about—so I could buy you out and then come to you as a man of means. And that's the only reason I entertained R.J.'s offer. How could I make an honest proposal of marriage if I owe you money? All our lives you'd wonder if the debt motivated me." He shook his head. "I can't have my wife wondering that."

A strangled sound, entirely inarticulate, emanated from her throat.

"You see? When my bank account didn't grow fast enough, I doubled my work. For you, Lucy. I did it to keep you. Now you want to run off, go to the big city and leave me and Cricket." He looked down at his callused palms, his features stiff and stark. "I can't pay you back yet. But if you'll have me, I swear I will. I'll work more than ever, you'll see."

Heart pounding in her ears so loudly she could barely hear, Lucy found herself incapable of speech. She felt dizzy and light-headed until she realized she'd stopped breathing and gulped air. She swayed, head beginning to clear. Everything inside her wanted to give him what he asked for.

"*Rusty,*" she whispered. Taking one jerky step forward, she touched his arm. "Rusty, I love you. Don't you know that? I've always loved you."

The man she adored closed his eyes as if sending up a prayer of thanks. His lashes rested like black fringe on his cheeks, and she thought he'd never looked so handsome, or so sweet.

In a heated rush his strong arms closed around her and she was warm again. As warm as she'd ever been in her entire life. Crushing her to him, he buried his face in her neck, mumbled words she couldn't discern, but in her womanly core she knew the essence of their meaning. She felt her mouth stretching wide in a radiant smile, her love spilling forth along with her tears. She hugged him back, laughing in joy.

"You're mine," he muttered, dropping ardent kisses on her throat, her ear, her cheeks and forehead. "Mine. You can't leave me. I won't allow it. You're my partner, dammit." He held her away and his manner became earnest. "I'm not Kenneth, Lucy. I won't browbeat you into anything. I couldn't do that. But I'll love you every day of my life. I love you, woman. Understand?"

Placing a tender hand on his cheek, she smiled into his eyes. It was hard to accept, to believe that her dream was, indeed, coming true. "I understand."

"You can have your dude ranch—you won't get more resistance from me. I don't care about that anymore. I just want you—"

"No," she said. "No dude ranch. I realize now what it would mean to you, having strangers stomping around, wrecking things."

One side of his mouth curved up. "Ornery female. I'm giving you what you want."

"You're giving me…yourself?" she teased.

He chuckled. "That, too. But how about a compromise? What if we just have a few people at a time, say two or three? Maybe make the place a sanctuary for women married to men like Kenneth.''

She thought about that. ''Do you mean, sort of a retreat for abused women?''

He lifted a shoulder. ''I don't know what you'd call it. But if we could give them a place to think, somewhere secure to go for a while. You've always said it helped you. And keeping the numbers down won't upset the routine on the ranch.'' Pausing, he carefully considered his next words. ''My father always told my brothers and me to keep the land pure, keep it private. He was a hard man, but not an unsympathetic one. If he were alive, I don't think he'd mind us sheltering a few people in need.''

''Yes,'' she said slowly, ''it's a wonderful idea. A fabulous idea. Maybe my original conception was too big, too...grandiose. And I never thought about helping verbally or physically abused women. But it could work. We could have a licensed therapist or doctor on call. We might teach them tools for dealing with their lives.'' Her mind whirling with possibilities, the words spilled out. The entire world seemed to open up; the whole Nevada sky and all its shimmering stars were the limit.

It was a testament, she thought in elation, of his regard for her. The project she so wanted and he'd long abhorred, he now lay at her feet like a gift.

''So will you?'' Rusty cut in. His arms squeezed her. She gazed at him, puzzled.

''Will you?'' he asked again, and this time she heard the desperate note in his voice. Slowly it dawned on her what he was asking. Heart full of love, Lucy realized that the brusque man was proposing to her in the only way he knew how.

Feeling deliciously brazen, she wound her arms around his neck and pulled him down for the kiss of his life.

"Will I ever," she whispered against his lips.

Epilogue

For the wedding Lucy wore a Western, ivory lace gown and matching cowboy boots with scalloped tops. She smiled so much her cheeks hurt.

During the prior weeks, she and Rusty had had several friendly arguments about the arrangements. He'd wanted to rent a formal hall in Lovelock, while she'd insisted their vows be exchanged right there on the ranch. In compromise, more on Rusty's part than hers, they settled on bringing Lovelock to them. Tables, chairs, peaked tent and a great arched gazebo, twined with greenery and rose blooms, were hauled in by a smiling hotel owner. He'd even brought propane heaters—to keep everyone toasty in the chilly winter air. Everything was organized on the grass, which Lucy insisted on mowing herself the day before.

Now a beaming Fritzy as well as Harris, who'd trimmed his mustache nearly by half in honor of the occasion, stood up for them. Beatrice and all the cowboys and ranchers for miles around had come to pay their respects. A four-piece band played soft ballads, then struck up a country version of the wedding march.

Poised before the preacher, Lucy cradled a gurgling Cricket in her arms while a proud Rusty in his ebony tuxedo, bolo tie and boots kept his hand on her back and didn't once leave her side. The special magnetism that defined him was more powerful than ever, she thought in pride. His smile was warm and intimate and never before had she felt so wanted or so loved.

After the ceremony, Lucy handed Cricket over to Fritzy. She and Rusty had already started legal adoption proceedings for the baby, and their lawyer assured them the mother was more than willing to give up all parental rights.

Now, as a married couple, she and Rusty spent an hour greeting their guests, then moved to a shadowed corner of the tent to share a private moment. "I love you," she whispered against his lips.

"Love you more," he whispered back. "When I think how close I came to losing you, it scares the hell out of me." For shattered seconds his face turned bleak and grim. "What would I do without you?"

Gently Lucy stroked his cheek. "You'll never need to find out." From the corner of her eye, she spotted Harris and Beatrice lingering together to one side, and nudged Rusty to look.

"You don't come into my diner much, do you? Why is that?" they heard Bea say. The woman ran a speculative eye up and down Harris's tall body.

The foreman's attention was instantly riveted. "Didn't know you were interested. Maybe I'll make it by more often."

"Interested?" she barked. "How could a woman tell what a handsome devil you are with all that hair covering your face? It's amazing what a good barber can do." She softened her sharp tone by reaching out to fuss with his collar. "You know, Harris, you need a keeper."

"That I do, Miss Beatrice," he agreed enthusiastically. "And if it'd please you, I'd shave every bit of hair right off my face."

A born coquette, Bea tilted her head in the age-old manner of a flirting woman. As she smiled, her teeth gleamed white and didn't seem quite so protruding. "You come on over to the diner for breakfast tomorrow."

He swallowed convulsively, as if unable to believe his luck. "Is sunrise all right?"

Rusty and Lucy burst out laughing. Yet Bea and Harris, so wrapped up in each other, didn't notice.

Lucy turned in her husband's strong arms. He grinned into her eyes, his own a warm, gleaming amber. At last, she thought in wonderment and joy, at last she had found a safe haven for herself.

And she might never have to climb a tree again.

* * * * *

Steeple Hill is proud to present
readers with this reader-favorite story
from bestselling author

Diana Palmer....

BLIND PROMISES

Diana Palmer fans will not be disappointed with
this Love Inspired® release about a nurse who
teaches the power of healing—and the
power of love—to a man who has
become hardened after a
tragic accident changes
his life forever.

**Don't miss BLIND PROMISES
in May 1999 from**

 *Love Inspired*®

Available at your favorite retail outlet.

ILIBP

Looking For More Romance?

Visit Romance.net

Look us up on-line at: http://www.romance.net

Check in daily for these and other exciting features:

Hot off the press

View all current titles, and purchase them on-line.

What do the stars have in store for you?

Horoscope

Hot deals

Exclusive offers available only at Romance.net

Plus, don't miss our interactive quizzes, contests and bonus gifts.

PWEB

CATCH THE BOUQUET!

These delightful stories of love and passion, by three of the romance world's bestselling authors, will make you look back on your own wedding with a smile—or give you some ideas for a future one!

THE MAN SHE MARRIED

by

ANN MAJOR

EMMA DARCY

ANNETTE BROADRICK

Available at your favorite retail outlet.

Look us up on-line at: http://www.romance.net   PSBR599

SOMETIMES THE SMALLEST PACKAGES CAN LEAD TO THE BIGGEST SURPRISES!

February 1999
A VOW, A RING, A BABY SWING
by Teresa Southwick (SR #1349)

Pregnant and alone, Rosie Marchetti had just been stood up at the altar. So family friend Steve Schafer stepped up the aisle and married her. Now Rosie is trying to convince him that this family was meant to be....

May 1999
THE BABY ARRANGEMENT
by Moyra Tarling (SR #1368)

Jared McAndrew has been searching for his son, and when he discovers Faith Nelson with his child he demands she come home with him. Can Faith convince Jared that he has the wrong mother—but the right bride?

Enjoy these stories of love and family. And look for future
BUNDLES OF JOY titles from Leanna Wilson and Suzanne McMinn
coming in the fall of 1999.

BUNDLES OF JOY
only from

▼Silhouette®

Available wherever Silhouette books are sold.

Look us up on-line at: http://www.romance.net

SRBOJJ-J

Coming in June 1999 from

Silhouette Books...

Those matchmaking folks at Gulliver's Travels are at it again—and look who they're working their magic on this time, in

HOLIDAY
Honeymoons

Two Tickets to Paradise

For the first time anywhere, enjoy these two new complete stories in one sizzling volume!

HIS FIRST FATHER'S DAY　　　Merline Lovelace

A little girl's search for her father leads her to Tony Peretti's front door…and leads *Tony* into the arms of his long-lost love—the child's mother!

MARRIED ON THE FOURTH　　　Carole Buck

Can summer love turn into the real thing? When it comes to Maddy Malone and Evan Blake's Independence Day romance, the answer is a definite "yes!"

Don't miss this brand-new release—
HOLIDAY HONEYMOONS: Two Tickets to Paradise—
coming June 1999, only from Silhouette Books.

Available at your favorite retail outlet.

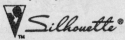

Look us up on-line at: http://www.romance.net　　　　　PSHH